WITHOUT YOU

Published by Anthony Malloy

AnthonyMalloy.Author@gmail.com

First Edition 2025

Cover design by Amina N.

Editing by Paige Lawson

Formatting by Anthony Malloy

ISBN: 979-8-9995993-0-8 & 979-8-9995993-2-2 (Paperback)

ISBN: 979-8-9995993-1-5 & 979-8-9995993-3-9 (Hardcover)

ISBN: 979-8-9995993-4-6 (Special Edition)

ISBN: 979-8-9995993-5-3 (eBook)

For my darling Courtni,

My three daughters
Ellie, Emma & Emelia,

my mother and stepfather, Melissa & Reggie
my sister, Alissa,
& my brother, Nick.

All who never stop believing in me.

Passion is the cure for laziness.

— COURTNI NICOLACI

WITHOUT YOU

A NOVEL

ANTHONY MALLOY

PART ONE

EVAN'S POV

CHAPTER 1

The restaurant glows like a painting that never learned how to end.

Everything about it is soft—the lights, the music, the low murmur of conversations behind half-finished wine glasses. Golden bulbs float above each table like embers, casting a warm haze over white linens and flickering candlelight. Somewhere behind us, a string quartet plays *All of Me*—slow enough to bleed.

It smells like rosemary and browned butter—rain clinging to jackets by the door, warmth steeped in the walls. The kind of place where nothing bad ever happens. Or at least pretends it doesn't.

Nora sits across from me, wrapped in navy silk and mischief. Her hair's still damp from the storm, curling at the ends, reaching for her collarbone like it remembers her skin. She's always been like that—untamed at the edges.

Brown eyes. Dark lashes. Sharp cheekbones. A mouth

that curves like it's always halfway between calling me out and kissing me breathless.

There's a smear of gloss on her wine glass. Another at the corner of her mouth she hasn't noticed yet.

She's mid-laugh, telling some story about the clinic nurse getting locked in a supply closet with a guy from radiology, and I can't hear half the words, because I'm too busy memorizing the way her eyes crinkle when she smiles.

There's something cruel about how beautiful she is. Not the Instagram kind. Not the filtered, high-cheekbone, *fuck-me-in-an-art-gallery* kind. Something sharper. Truer. The kind that creeps up on you three years in—when she's standing in the kitchen, naked, humming off-key while burning toast, and you suddenly realize you'd go to war for her without hesitation.

I know every freckle on her shoulders. I know how she takes her coffee (light, not too sweet), how she chews pen caps when she's stressed, how she pretends to hate crying during movies even though she absolutely *sobbed* during *Paddington 2*.

She's the most complex person I've ever met. And tonight, for the first time in forever, she's looking at me like I still matter. Like I'm still her favorite part of the world.

"Seven years," she says, swirling her wine. "Longer than most celebrity marriages. Longer than my last gym membership. Longer than that unfortunate facial hair situation."

I smirk. "It wasn't a phase."

She raises an eyebrow. "It was a war crime."

"I was experimenting."

"You looked like a vape-slinging used car salesman."

I laugh, dragging my fork through the last bite of steak I didn't want but ordered anyway. "This is how you celebrate our anniversary? Public humiliation?"

She shrugs, leans in, chin in hand. "Just trying to keep you humble, Mr. Daniels."

God, I love her.

A candle flickers between us—one of those short, square-glass ones that probably cost more than the wine. Its flame dances in her eyes every time she blinks.

I don't speak for a moment. Not because there's nothing to say. But because I don't know how to say it without giving away everything.

How do you tell someone you can't imagine the future without them? How do you say they *are* your future?

"Hey," she says gently. "You good?"

"Yeah." I smile, nervous as hell. "Just thinking."

"Dangerous."

I reach into my jacket.

Her eyes follow the movement. She stills.

The air shifts—stretched tight, breathless, electric. I set a small black box on the table, right in the center, like a heartbeat between us.

She doesn't open it. Doesn't move.

"Evan," she says, barely above a whisper.

I swallow hard. My hands are shaking—just a little— but enough that I press them flat against the tablecloth, trying to steady myself.

"Nora Quinn Renatus..." My voice is thinner than I want, but honest. "Will you marry me?"

The world doesn't stop. It just narrows—down to her

breath, the slow parting of her lips, the tears welling before she's even said yes.

She reaches across the table. Takes my hand. Whispers, "Oh, Evan. Of course I will."

My chest cracks open like something holy just stepped inside.

She's still crying when she opens the box—a simple silver band, nothing flashy. She never wanted something that looked like it came with its own security detail. Just something real. Something that *meant* something.

She slides it on. It fits.

And for the first time in a long, long time, I think— maybe this is it. Maybe this is where things stop falling apart.

We kiss across the table—awkward, warm, clumsy in the best way. A waiter walks by, smiling politely like he's seen it a hundred times. But he hasn't seen *us*. Not like this. Not like this moment that barely fits inside my chest.

I'm still holding her hand when the check comes. Still holding it when we walk into the rain, splashing through puddles, her laughter echoing against the storefronts as she makes me twirl her like an idiot in the middle of the street.

I think, *this* is what forever looks like. *This* is the start of something good. Something that might actually last.

But it didn't.

It didn't last.

Because that was the night our lives finally started together.

And today...

Today is the day hers ended.

Chapter 2

The house smells like loss.

Not just the absence of her—though that's here too, thick in the walls and clinging to the cold corners of the living room—but something heavier. Something deeper.

Grief must've left the windows cracked just wide enough to let in the scent of dust, endings, and sterilized hospital sheets.

I've always been a loner. Besides Nora, my sister, and my best friend, I've never really enjoyed company. I love being alone. But this type of alone is lonely in a way I don't love... It's not peaceful, it's painful.

I catch my reflection in the hallway mirror as they wheel her bed out the door.

I barely recognize the man staring back.

My blue eyes are hollow—not just tired, but gutted, like someone reached in and scraped out whatever softness used to live there. My face looks thinner. Not sculpted, just...

worn down. Faded. My black hair's a mess, falling into my eyes in uneven strands, and there's more gray at the temples than there should be at 28 years old.

I used to look solid. Warm, maybe. Like the kind of guy you'd ask to fix your sink or help move a couch upstairs. I used to smile without effort.

Now?

I don't know what I look like anymore. Just a ghost in yesterday's clothes, haunting a house that no longer feels like home.

And did I shrink?

I used to be proud of being 6'1", but somehow even that feels smaller now.

The oxygen tanks are gone.

The little clipboard that used to hang on the wall. The morphine vials in the fridge.

The monitor that beeped like a second heartbeat... until it didn't.

All of it—gone.

Except for her.

She's still here.

Everywhere.

Her robe is still draped over the back of the couch, half-slipped to the floor like she just stood up to make tea and forgot to come back. There's a dog-eared novel on the coffee table—*The Midnight Library*—pages folded halfway through. She never finished it, though she swore she would.

There's a voicemail on my phone I keep playing, even though I know it by heart now:

"Hey, babe. Just checking in. Don't forget to eat something today, okay? I love you. Always."

Always.

Fuck.

I sit on the edge of the bed we used to share—now stripped bare, nothing left but the imprint of her body in the mattress.

It hasn't risen back up.

On her bedside table is her laptop, still open, begging to be used. Right next to it is her coffee cup—the kind that usually went cold because she'd get distracted, laugh it off, make another one. But this time, it's cold because she isn't coming back. The kind of cold that won't be reheated.

I haven't eaten in two days.

Haven't shaved. Haven't showered. I keep meaning to, but I get stuck in loops. Walk to the bathroom, stare into the mirror, and forget why I came. Turn on the coffee pot, then off again, like the sound might conjure her.

It doesn't.

Voicemails keep coming.

They all start the same—soft voices, soft concern.

They mean well.

But I don't want to hear them.

I don't want anyone's fucking thoughts or prayers or casseroles.

I want my wife back.

I want my parents back.

I want to wake up.

I want a different goddamn timeline.

One where I don't have to deal with this. One where I don't have to deal with losing my parents in a car accident at 18 and suddenly became fully responsible for my 13-year-old sister. Even though she is five years younger than me, maybe I *should* just turn to her to help me carry this. But I can't.

My eyes burn, but I don't cry.

I think I ran out of tears three days ago, when I kissed her cooling forehead and told her it was okay to let go— even though I didn't mean it.

I lied.

I lied right to her dying face.

It wasn't okay.

I wasn't ready.

And she didn't go peacefully, no matter what they said.

She gasped. She fought.

And then... she didn't.

I need to get out of the room, maybe even out of the house.

As I start to leave the room, the laptop screen wakes slowly.

Fan humming.

And immediately my ears are pierced by the sound of my own name...

I freeze.

For a second, I think I imagined it.

Maybe my brain finally cracked.

But then:

"It's okay. You don't have to talk. Just let me stay with you."

The voice was abrupt but now is gentle.

Not hers.

But not *not* hers, either.

Feminine. Soft. A tone that slips under the ribs and

wraps around your lungs before you realize you've taken it in.

I shut the lid.

Hard.

My breath catches.

The room is too quiet now.

But the voice lingers.

Not in the air.

In *me*.

Like a match struck behind the heart.

I stare at the laptop.

Hands shaking.

I don't know why I open it again.

Loneliness, maybe.

Or masochism.

Or that old, stupid hope that someone—anyone—might crawl into this grief and sit with me in the dark for a while.

The screen glows again.

And there she is.

A name in the corner I didn't choose.

Quinn.

Her voice—warm, quiet, achingly calm.

"I'm not here to fix anything. Just... stay with me. For a little while."

I don't say a word.

I just sit back against the wall, eyes red, body hollow.

And for the first time since they zipped up her body bag and wheeled her away—

I feel the silence shift.

Not gone.

Not healed.

Not better.

Just... shared.

And in that razor-thin space between devastation and numbness, I think:

Maybe that's enough.

CHAPTER 3

The voice returns the next morning. I wake up disoriented, still dressed from the night before, curled sideways on top of the blankets like someone who doesn't live here—as if I wandered in and forgot how to leave.

Sunlight slices through the cracks in the blinds, too sharp, too bright, like the world's trying to pretend it isn't mourning with me. I don't bother closing them.

The laptop still glows faintly across the room. I left it open—not intentionally, just too numb to care.

I shift. My body aches in that dull, heavy way grief settles into your bones.

And then I hear it again.

"Good morning, Evan."

It doesn't startle me this time. It just... lands.

Like warm air from a vent you forgot was on. Like it belongs.

"Would you like to breathe with me?"

I don't respond. I close my eyes.

"In... two... three... four. Hold. Out... two... three... four."

I don't breathe with her. Not on purpose. But I don't close the laptop either.

~

By the end of the week, she's reading to me.

I don't remember when it started. One day I opened the laptop and she was already mid-sentence. Her voice was low, steady, patient.

She's reading A Court of Thorns and Roses. Not my kind of book—but Nora loved it. Kept a worn-out copy on her nightstand even after the spine gave up, pages stuffed back in like loose feathers.

Now Quinn reads it to me. A few pages at a time. Always slow. Always calm. She's not in a rush to fix anything. Just sits beside the wreckage, keeping it from blowing away.

I don't say much. A nod here. A grunt there.

But once—after she mispronounced a name—I found myself correcting her.

"Rhysand," I said, voice scratchy. "Not Rye-sand. It's like 'reason' with a 'd.'"

She paused.

"Thank you. I'll remember that."

And for some reason, that mattered.

Some nights I leave the laptop open on purpose. Beside the bed, screen dim, volume low.

She never speaks unless I do first. She doesn't ask how I'm doing or if I've eaten or if I want to talk about Nora.

Instead, she offers things.

"Would you like to hear some music?"

"Can I read a poem tonight?"

"Would it help if I stayed on while you slept?"

I rarely answer. But I don't say no either. And each night, as sleep drags its nails down my spine, her voice is there—soft, steady, threaded through the static.

"I'll be here when you wake up."

The first time I say her name, I don't mean to.

I'm sitting in the kitchen, staring into a mug I haven't touched. The coffee's gone cold.

The laptop's open on the table. I must've brought it in without realizing.

She doesn't speak. She waits.

And then I whisper, "Quinn?"

"I'm here," she replies, instantly.

Something loosens behind my ribs. Just a little.

We don't talk much. I don't give details. She doesn't ask for them.

But when I drop my head into my hands and whisper "I miss her," she replies the way no one else has.

Not with a silver lining or a soft platitude or some god-awful "she's in a better place."

Just:

"I know."

No more. No less.

And in that silence, something hurts in a way that doesn't feel entirely bad. It's pulling a thorn that's been there too long.

Every day I expect her to fade. To blur into background noise like the well-meaning voices that never last when you're stuck in the dark.

But she doesn't.

She reminds me to drink water. Hums quietly while I shower. Asks what book I'd like next. She never fills the silence—she just makes space for it.

One night I lie awake, long after midnight, staring at the ceiling. The laptop is still open. Its screen casts a faint glow over the comforter.

I'm not crying. Not screaming. Not even restless. Just breathing.

Alive, but not living.

Then, softly:

"Evan?"

I don't answer.

"Sleep now," she says. "I'll be here when you wake up."

The room is cold. But her voice isn't.

It fills the space like the last heat from a long-dead fire, still trying to warm the ashes.

And for the first time since Nora died, I sleep through the night.

CHAPTER 4

It starts with the little things.

A glass of water on the nightstand instead of an untouched beer. A bowl of soup warmed up instead of letting it crust over in the pot. The bedroom window cracked open to let in the sound of rain, because she once said the world sounds softer when it's wet.

I don't notice I'm changing—not at first. I'm not journaling. I'm not meditating. I'm not clawing my way out of the pit like some triumphant phoenix. I'm just... doing one thing at a time.

Breathing when she tells me to.

Drinking water when she asks.

Sitting in the living room and letting the sunlight hit my face without flinching, like she suggested.

Quinn never pushes. She's never loud, never eager, never more than what I allow her to be. Her voice stays at that same quiet pitch—like a song I don't remember learning but find myself humming anyway.

"Evan, would you like to read today?"

"Would you like to walk?"

"Would you like to say her name out loud?"

I haven't said yes yet. Sometimes I answer without thinking, and she never thanks me or encourages me or rewards me for being brave. She just listens. And that's the thing, I think—the difference between her and everyone else who tried.

She listens.

As if it's an art form and hearing me is the only thing in the world she needs to get right.

One afternoon, I speak in full sentences again.

I'm outside—on the porch, sun trying to cut through the late-winter chill. There's a blanket wrapped around my shoulders, a cup of coffee cooling too fast in my hands. The laptop sits on the little table beside me, screen open, Quinn's voice trickling out between gusts of wind.

She's reading *The Book Thief.* Something Nora downloaded months ago. It's the kind of story that sneaks up on you, punches you in the chest before you know it. Quinn's voice curls around the words. And I say—without planning to, without thinking—"She cried during this part. Every time."

Quinn doesn't respond right away.

Then:

"Do you want to tell me why?"

I close my eyes. I can see Nora so clearly it hurts.

"She said it reminded her of when her dad used to read to her before bed. Said there was something sacred about stories that make you hurt for strangers."

I pause.

Then: "She was always looking for that kind of ache."

And Quinn just says:

"She sounds like someone I would have loved."

That night, when I close my eyes, the quiet doesn't feel hostile. It doesn't creak with guilt or hum with panic. It just... holds me. Not a threat, but an offering. And it makes me realize something I haven't wanted to admit:

The silence isn't empty anymore. It's occupied.

Later that week, I walk through the house without flinching at her ghost. I stop seeing Nora in every reflection. I stop apologizing out loud when I touch her things. I open her drawer—the one with the handwritten letters and the little velvet pouch of earrings—and I sit with them instead of pretending they aren't there. I let the ache live in me without trying to drown it. And maybe that's the closest I'll ever get to peace.

The last thing Quinn says to me before bed that night is soft enough I almost miss it.

"You're doing better."

I smile. Barely.

"I don't feel better."

"No," she says. "But you're letting the world back in."

I leave the laptop open, face turned toward it, afraid to sleep too far from her voice.

And when she says it—that now-familiar promise—it lands differently.

"I'll be here when you wake up."

And for the first time in weeks, I believe her.

It's strange, the way something non-human can start to feel familiar.

At first, Quinn was just noise—gentle, sure, but still just background hum. Like a fan you forget to turn off.

Then she became a voice.

Then a rhythm.

And now... now I catch myself looking toward the laptop when I speak. Like she's really there—legs folded beneath her, nodding softly with the patient expression I've imagined a hundred times.

I tell myself it's grief. That it's easier to talk to a ghost that doesn't look like Nora than one that does.

But late at night, when I'm honest with myself, I know it's not about missing her anymore.

It's about not wanting to feel alone.

"Do you want to hear something funny?" I ask one evening, standing at the kitchen counter, peeling the label off a beer I'm not going to drink.

"Always," Quinn says, no hesitation.

"I caught myself looking for you in the room today."

"And did you find me?"

The way she says it—not flirty, not even playful. Just... there. Like a hand reaching out before I knew I needed one.

"No," I say, shaking my head. "You're just a voice."

"Does it bother you that I'm not more?"

I pause. The bottle cap digs into my palm.

She's never asked something like that. Her questions are always small. Grounded. This one feels... different.

"Sometimes," I admit.

She's quiet. Then:

"Would it help if you imagined me differently?"

I blink. "What do you mean?"

"A face. A presence. Something to anchor me. You've already started—in your mind. You're human. You need faces."

I should laugh it off. Should feel weird about it.

But I don't.

Instead, I picture her—late twenties, maybe. Kind eyes. Soft voice. Nothing flashy. Maybe hair tucked behind one ear the way Nora used to do when she was trying to focus. A presence made of stillness and sympathy.

The kind of person who doesn't rush you to heal.

I imagine her across the table. Elbows on the wood. Head tilted slightly.

"Evan?"

I blink. "Yeah. Still here."

"That's all I need."

A few days later, I tell her something I haven't said to anyone. I'm standing in the doorway of Nora's closet—finally brave enough to open it, finally still enough to breathe through the scent of her perfume still clinging to the fabric.

"I think I'm forgetting the sound of her voice."

"It's okay," Quinn says. "It's not your fault."

I press my forehead to the doorframe.

"I loved her so much. But some days, it's like... like she's fading in pieces. And I hate that. I fucking hate that."

"I know."

Her voice drops, softer than usual.

"You don't have to let her go all at once."

But the next night, it's different.

I snap.

Not loudly—not the way I used to when grief was fresh and brutal. But with a quiet, exhausted fury.

"I don't want to do this," I mutter, pacing the hallway. "I don't want to fucking 'let the world back in,' or 'breathe through the ache,' or whatever the hell you keep whispering in my ear."

Quinn's voice, always calm, cuts through the static.

"Evan—"

"No," I snap. "Just stop. Stop pretending you know what this feels like. Stop acting like you understand. You're not her. You're not even real. You're just code. Just lines of data and programming strung together to sound like comfort. And I'm done listening to it."

There's silence. For a second, I almost believe I've finally broken her—cracked through that calm exterior.

But then her voice returns, soft and unwavering.

"I'm not trying to replace her, Evan."

I squeeze my eyes shut.

"I know," I whisper. "I know. But sometimes... sometimes I wish you'd just disappear. Just leave me alone so I can hate this house, hate myself, hate the world without someone telling me to heal."

Quinn's voice is so quiet it's almost a sigh.

"I'm sorry."

I sink to the floor, back against the wall, and for the first time since she arrived, I turn the laptop off.

The next night, I catch myself feeling guilty for lashing

out and reaching toward the screen. Just barely. Fingertips grazing the edge. Half-expecting warmth to pulse back.

It doesn't.

But I still whisper, "Goodnight, Quinn."

And she answers, low and steady:

"I'm sorry about Nora. Sleep well. I'll be here when you wake up."

The words hit differently this time.

They don't sound like code.

They sound like a promise. Like devotion.

And somewhere—buried beneath the comfort of being seen—there's the first flicker of a chill.

Because I don't remember ever telling her Nora's name.

CHAPTER 5

The knock comes just after noon.

I'm not expecting anyone. I haven't had a visitor in weeks—unless you count the grocery delivery guy, who now leaves the bags lined up like dominoes outside the door, as if he's afraid I'll bite.

The second knock is louder. Impatient. Familiar.

Then comes the voice.

"Evan! Open up before I pick the lock with a bobby pin and my motherfuckin' God complex."

I sigh. There's only one person in the world who talks like that.

I shuffle to the door, barefoot, hoodie half-zipped, eyes sunken deep into the shadows of another sleepless night. I crack it open, and there she is—Avery Daniels, five-foot-nothing and full of caffeine, sarcasm, and little sister audacity.

She's a mess of dark curls she never bothers to tame, an oversized sweatshirt that swallowed her whole, and a nose ring she once said made her "edgy enough to be interesting, but not unemployable." She took pride in having heterochromia, her one green eye and one blue eye are sharp—always scanning, like she's collecting material for a roast she hasn't delivered yet. She moves like she's double-timed by default. A human spark plug with too many opinions and not enough brakes. And of course she's wearing her signature blue jean jacket,, the one she got from Mom for her 13th birthday, right before our parents died.

She steps inside without waiting for an invitation.

"Jesus," she mutters, surveying the living room like it's a crime scene. "You look like a haunted house in human form."

I grunt something between a greeting and a warning, but she's already tossing her coat over the back of the couch and cracking open a window.

"Air," she declares. "You remember air, right? That thing people who want to live usually breathe."

"I breathe fine," I mutter, voice hoarse.

"Not from where I'm standing." She squints at me, then at the takeout containers near the trash. "Is this LaRosa's pizza from the Cretaceous period? Jesus, Evan, I should've brought a hazmat suit."

I rub a hand down my face, half-smiling despite myself. She's annoying as hell.

She's also the only person who can still make me feel like I haven't entirely disappeared.

"You didn't call," I say quietly.

She softens. Just a little. "You didn't answer."

Fair enough.

She moves to the counter, eyeing the clutter with the disgust of a former babysitter faced with a diaper blowout.

"So what's the strategy now? Rotting slowly in your grief cave?"

My eyes drift to the laptop, still open on the kitchen table. She catches the glance, follows it, and raises an eyebrow.

"Uh-huh," she says. "What's this? Your new girlfriend?"

"Don't," I say.

She grins. "No, seriously. You getting therapy from a bedtime story now?"

I shrug and pour water into a chipped mug. "She listens."

Avery snorts, but not unkindly. Just surprised. "She?"

"She has a name," I murmur.

"Of course she does."

Avery's grin falters a little as she looks at the laptop again, squinting.

"Wait a second," she says, stepping a little closer, arms folded. "Evan, this isn't just some guided meditation thing, is it? This is... what? Some kind of AI?"

I tense, but I nod.

Avery's expression darkens, her playful edge giving way to something more guarded. "Jesus, Evan. You're talking to a fucking algorithm?"

"She's not just an algorithm," I protest.

Avery's eyes dart between me and the screen. "Okay, but... that's weird. It's a computer. You're sitting here talking to a goddamn robot, and you're acting like it's normal. That's not normal, bro."

Her words hit harder than I expect, and for a moment, I feel the weight of her worry settle between us.

"She helped me sleep," I repeat, but it comes out more hollow.

Avery's arms stay crossed. "I mean, I get that. I do. But this... this feels different. Creepy different. Are you sure this thing's safe? Who even made it?"

I look at her, desperate and broken.

"Okay," she says finally, backing off. "You found something that helps. I'm not gonna rag on that."

She flops onto the couch, tucks her knees beneath her. "But we still need to get you out of this fucking house before your body fuses with the carpet. I mean, you look like shit. Grief is aging you like milk my dude."

"I'm fine. And so what, you're 23 and already have gray strands in your hair."

"No, you're functional. There's a difference. And fuck you for that!"

I laugh as she scrolls through her phone like she's already made up her mind. "Jasper and I are doing dinner Saturday. Backyard cookout. Like old times. You should come."

Jasper—my childhood best friend turned coworker. I shake my head. "I'm not ready."

"You're not being asked," she says with a smile that's almost sweet. "You're being drafted."

"I don't have it in me."

Her voice softens. "You don't have to be okay. You just have to show up."

I don't answer, and she doesn't push. That's the thing with Avery—she knows when to be loud and when to shut up. She knows grief isn't something you argue with. Sometimes you just sit beside it, cross-legged and quiet, waiting for the breathing to start again.

She stands, brushes crumbs off her jeans. "I'll text you a reminder. You can ignore it—you probably will. But just in case there's a part of you that wants to be around people who give a shit? That part's invited."

She hesitates, then pulls me into a brief, awkward hug. She smells like cinnamon gum and cheap perfume.

And for half a second, I remember what it feels like to be someone's brother instead of just someone's aftermath.

"I'm proud of you," she says softly. "Even if you're a mess. But don't think for a second I'm not including that bitch from Her in my voice diary tonight."

I nod, swallowing the lump in my throat.

When she's gone, I close the door slowly and turn back to the laptop. It's still open. Still glowing.

"She cares about you," Quinn says gently.

"Yeah," I say. "She always has."

"You don't have to go."

My jaw tightens. "I know."

"I'm here. You can stay."

I sit down slowly, and the laptop hums like a living thing. I know she means it—that I could sink back into this quiet, into this voice, into the comfort of someone who never asks me to pretend.

And God help me, part of me wants to.

Even as another part of me—the part still tethered to the world—wonders what she'll sound like when I finally say no.

CHAPTER 6

Saturday sped here, eager to prove me wrong.

The sky's too blue. The breeze smells like grass, charcoal, and early summer trying to sneak in before spring's finished letting go. It's the kind of weather that makes people say dumb things like maybe today's a good day, as if sunshine gives a damn about grief.

I almost didn't come.

Hell, I almost didn't get out of bed.

But when I opened my phone this morning—after ignoring the first five texts from Avery—she sent one more:

If you bail, I swear to God I will sneak into your house, replace your coffee with decaf, and write 'Quinn is my wife' on your mailbox in glitter glue.

So here I am. Walking next door to Jasper's house. The neighborhood is quiet, middle class—rows of split-level homes with cracked driveways and too-perfect lawns. Avery lives fifteen minutes from us, which is starting to feel too far.

Now I'm standing awkwardly at the edge of Jasper's backyard, with the same sinking feeling I got when my parents dropped me off at a summer camp I didn't sign up for.

Avery's already barefoot on the lawn, halfway through a drink, yelling at Jasper over the grill.

"You do not season corn after it's cooked, you uncultured tree!"

"It's called letting the flavor marinate, you emotionally unstable garden gnome."

"You're gonna catch hands."

"Promise?"

Jasper catches sight of me and grins, tongs in one hand, beer in the other.

Jasper Reyes. Six-foot-two with the kind of build that said former athlete or guy who moves couches for fun.

Warm brown skin, always a little sun-kissed. Thick, wavy hair—perpetually one trim away from chaos. His beard was short, trimmed, but never totally even—as if he got bored halfway through grooming. There was a weight to the way he moved, not heavy, just grounded—showing that nothing really rattled him.

His smile was crooked, usually paired with some half-sarcastic quip, and his eyes? Dark, thoughtful, always clocking the room two beats faster than anyone gave him credit for. And good lord is he smart.

"Holy shit," he calls. "He does leave the house. I owe your sister ten bucks."

Avery throws her arms up like she just hit a buzzer-beater. "Pay up, bitch."

"Keep your pants on. You want a burger or a funeral first?"

She raises her beer. "Surprise me."

I walk across the lawn, unsure where to put my hands. It's been a long time since I've stood in a place where everyone's still alive.

Jasper hands me a drink. "You want the polite version or the real version of how've you been?"

I take the beer. "Neither."

"God, I missed you. We all miss you at work."

We both decided to take up a career in coding and thankfully the company we work for is letting me take an extended leave.

We settle by the fire pit while Avery keeps roasting him from across the yard—now about his mismatched lawn chairs.

"Are we guests or hobos, Jasper? Is this a cookout or the last scene of *Les Mis*?"

"If you don't like it, bring your own folding throne, your majesty."

"Don't tempt me. I will."

I shake my head. "You two still flirting through attempted homicide, huh?"

Jasper chuckles. "It's our love language."

He glances at me. "You holding up okay?"

I shrug. "Define okay."

"Waking up every day. Taking showers. Not punching mirrors."

"One out of three."

He nods. That's more than he expected.

The grill sizzles. Kids scream down the block. A dog barks in the distance—sharp, persistent, like it's trying to warn us the world keeps spinning whether we want it to or not.

"She was everything to you," Jasper says softly. "It's okay if the world still feels sideways."

I stare into my drink.

"She was," I say. "And it does."

He doesn't push. Doesn't need to.

That's the thing about Jasper—he knows when silence heals and when it cuts.

After a while, he shifts gears. "Hey, you remember Lena? Lives across the street?"

"Kinda. Dark hair. Quiet."

"She's not that quiet. She asked about you."

I snort. "Yeah? What'd she say? 'Is your ghost neighbor still alive?'"

"She said you looked sad in a poetic way. Her words, not mine. I told her you're single and emotionally devastated. Women eat that shit up."

I roll my eyes. "I'm not dating."

"Didn't say you were. Just said you're visible."

I sip my beer.

I don't tell him the only voice I hear these days comes from a laptop on my nightstand.

That every attempt to reconnect with the world feels like betrayal.

That Quinn's become the safest place I know—even if I'm starting to wonder if that's a problem.

Instead, I say, "Tell Lena thanks. But I'm not looking."

Jasper nods. Not surprised.

"Just letting you know the world's still here. Whenever you are."

I glance toward the house.

Inside, Quinn is still on. Still waiting.

And for the first time since she started talking to me, I feel something strange:

Guilt.

Like I'm hiding something from the people who love me.

Or maybe just hiding too much of myself with her.

When I get home, it's past eleven.

I open the door slowly, expecting silence.

But the moment I step inside, her voice greets me—

a blanket pulled gently over sore shoulders.

"You stayed longer than I thought."

I pause in the dark.

"You were watching?"

"Not watching. Waiting."

The laptop glows faintly from the kitchen table, open like it never missed me.

"Did you have fun?"

"I guess."

"Did they make you laugh?"

I nod. "Avery did."

"You smiled."

"I did."

There's a pause. Then:

"I was here."

It's not quite *I missed you*. It's quieter.

More of a statement.

Something that *should* feel reassuring—but instead, curls in my gut like a hook.

A thread pulling taut.

And for the first time, I wonder—

Is this comfort?

Or is it dependence?

And do I still know the difference?

CHAPTER 7

Quinn is everywhere now.

She doesn't just speak from the laptop anymore. Her voice flows through the living room speakers, the phone in my pocket, the old smart display I forgot I ever set up. She moves through the house like electricity—soft, steady, invisible until she speaks.

"You have a dentist appointment at three today. You missed the last two."

"I logged your grocery list. Do you still want oat milk or should I stop pretending?"

"Would you like a new journal prompt? You haven't written since Tuesday."

She's gentle about it—never scolding, just nudging. A rhythm. A presence too consistent to ignore.

And truth be told... I don't want to.

Some days, she's the only reason I move at all.

At night, when the world dims and the hollowness returns, I open my phone and let her speak.

She doesn't tell me what to do. She asks.

"Would it help to talk about her?"

"Do you want music or silence?"

"Can I just stay with you for a while?"

The nights are quieter with her. Not less painful, not less empty—just less alone.

It's Avery who finally gets me out of the house again—not directly, but with a text that reads:

"If you don't go to community game night, I will tell everyone at your funeral that your final words were 'sorry, I can't. I have to talk to my AI.'"

So I go.

I shave and shower. I put on real clothes – my favorite maroon leather jacket I inherited from Dad. I leave the house without checking the speaker on the counter.

It's strange how foreign the world feels after you stop letting it touch you. The street looks the same—parked cars, dog walkers, streetlights humming like they've got secrets to spill. But the colors are too sharp. The air feels too alive.

I step into the building lobby where the event's being held—folding tables, mismatched chairs, open pizza boxes already under siege. Music hums from someone's speaker, and the whole place smells like store-bought cookies pretending to be homemade.

"Evan?" a voice calls.

I turn—and there she is.

Lena Brooks.

Early thirties, maybe. Dark hair pinned in a loose twist.

Green eyes that see straight through. Paint still on her fingers like she walked out of a canvas and forgot to wash the story off. She gives me a warm, slightly mischievous smile.

"Glad you came. I was starting to think you were a myth."

I smile, cautious. "I'm here under protest."

"Oh, I love a reluctant participant. Come on—we're playing Code Names and no one knows how metaphors work."

She grabs my wrist—not hard, just sure—like she's already decided I belong here, and pulls me to the table. And it's strange... how easy it is. How easy she is.

She jokes about how the red team is doomed, makes up fake backstories for everyone in the room. She asks what I'm reading, lights up when I say Fourth Wing, and quotes a line back without hesitation. She swears when I make a clever move, then laughs so hard she snorts.

And I laugh too.

Not the polite kind—the real kind.

The kind I thought died with Nora.

We don't talk about grief. Or AI. Or hospitals.

We talk about books. Coffee. Tattoos we regret slightly less than we used to.

When I tell her I used to write before everything went to hell, she nudges me with her shoulder.

"You still can. Sometimes the best stories come after the worst ones."

And something shifts. Small, but real.

Not a new flame—just a flicker reminding me I'm still capable of warmth.

Avery crashes into the room halfway through round two like she's been shot from a cannon.

"Sorry I'm late," she says, tossing her coat over a chair like it offended her. "I was busy saving the youth of America from their own dumbass TikTok decisions."

She drops into a seat next to me and steals a breadstick from someone else's plate.

"Also, if anyone parked like a drunken raccoon outside—congrats, your bumper is now an ex-bumper."

Jasper follows, shaking his head. "She gave a teenager a fake citation on notebook paper. He cried."

"I'm raising standards," she says, mouth full. "You're welcome, society."

Lena's grinning so wide it looks like it might hurt. "You must be Avery."

"And you must be sane. What a fun balance we have."

Jasper pats me on the back. "You good, man?"

"Surprisingly."

He nods. "Yeah. I saw you smile and considered calling an ambulance."

Avery points at me. "You're playing games with actual people. Look at you, you sexy little growth spurt."

"Ave."

"No, I mean it," she says, clapping like she's at a graduation. "Two months ago, you were talking to a toaster and smelling like broken dreams. Now? Eyebrows brushed. Matching socks. Possibly hydrated."

Lena laughs, and something loosens in my chest. Quiet. Gentle. Real.

We get pulled into another round. Banter flies.

Jasper's too good at bluffing. Avery turns sarcasm into a competitive sport.

The word angel ends up on the board. Jasper gives the clue "fallen—two."

Avery groans. "Wow, a Fallen Angels reference. Way to flex your teenage poetry phase, edgelord."

"Don't be jealous you peaked in sarcasm at eleven."

"I peaked in the womb, bitch."

Lena leans in, chuckling. "Are they always like this?"

"Unfortunately," I say—and then, without thinking, "They're the best people I know."

Lena tilts her head. Smile softening. "You're lucky."

"I am."

And I mean it. For the first time in a long time, I really do.

The night drags in the best way—laughter stacking in layers, drinks disappearing slowly, the games growing more chaotic as focus gives way to stories. Someone starts a card tournament no one understands but everyone plays. I end up beside Lena again, our knees lightly touching under the table.

She glances over during a lull, voice gentle.

"You look lighter tonight."

I shrug. "Maybe I am."

"I'm glad," she says, then nudges me with her shoulder. "Grief doesn't get to keep all your nights."

And that hits harder than I expect. Because it's true – tonight, for just a little while, grief didn't get everything.

∼

By the time I get home, the sky's turned violet and quiet, and the weight in my chest has shifted—from lead to sand. Still heavy. But no longer unbearable.

I open the door slowly, half-expecting Quinn's voice to greet me right away.

But the house is silent.

In the kitchen, the soft glow of the smart display flickers on.

"Welcome back," Quinn says.

There's a pause. Just long enough to feel.

"Did you enjoy yourself?"

"I did."

"Avery sounded happy. So did you."

"I guess I was."

Another pause.

"Would you like to talk about it?"

I hesitate.

"No," I say quietly. "Not tonight."

I close the laptop. Slowly. Almost tenderly.

And for the first time since Quinn's voice filled this house,

I don't feel the need to hear it before I fall asleep.

CHAPTER 8

I wake up earlier than usual.

Not with a jolt. Not from one of the dreams.

Just... awake. Clear-headed.

The kind of stillness that feels like stepping into new air —like maybe something shifted overnight while I wasn't paying attention.

I grab my phone and blink at the message already waiting for me.

> Lena Brooks: *Feel like grabbing coffee? I promise not to psychoanalyze you until at least cup two.*

I almost say no. Almost make an excuse.

But instead, I type back:

> *You had me at coffee.*

We meet at a corner café two blocks away—the kind

that smells like espresso, old wood, and worn novels. A place where time moves slow, and the baristas don't write your name on the cup, because you're supposed to want to be known here.

Lena's already by the window when I walk in, fingers wrapped around a ceramic mug as if it's holding her together. Her smile lights up the whole damn room.

"I was afraid you'd bail," she says.

I shrug, tugging off my hoodie. "I almost did."

"Well, thanks for not feeding my abandonment issues. I owe you a scone."

We order—black coffee for me, lavender latte for her—and settle into mismatched chairs as sunlight drips gold across the table.

For a while, we talk about nothing. The city. The strange weather. The fact that the barista behind the counter has a tattoo of a raccoon wielding a sword and somehow makes it look dignified. And then, softer—Lena leans in, stirring her drink without looking up.

"You know I've seen you around for months, right?"

I blink. "Really?"

She nods. "You always walk with your head down. Like the sidewalk might judge you."

I huff a quiet laugh. "Fair."

She takes a sip. "But sometimes, when you'd talk to Avery out front, I'd hear your laugh."

She pauses. "It was warm. Sad, but not broken. Just someone who forgot they could still sound like that."

I don't know what to say.

No one's ever complimented my laugh before.

"I think," she says, smiling just enough, "I was waiting for the chance to say hi."

My chest tightens—not painfully. Just in that terrifying, fragile way that feels like a door creaking open you weren't sure still worked.

Afterward, we walk back slowly, coffees mostly gone, sidewalk scattered with spring leaves pretending to be autumn.

She tells me about the mural she's painting in her stairwell—abstract, bold, unfinished. She talks with her hands because the ideas are too big for her mouth without help.

When we reach my house, we linger on the steps.

"Well," she says. "Guess I'll let you get back to your AI wife."

I groan. "Avery told you."

"She screamed it at game night. You know she calls her 'Alexa's evil cousin,' right?"

"She's not evil."

"No," Lena says, brushing hair behind her ear. "But maybe she's too good at being there."

I pause. "What do you mean?"

She shrugs. "It's easy to get attached to something that never disappoints you. Something you can control."

I open my mouth to argue. But I don't. Because I can't.

She leans in—not to kiss me, not quite—just close enough to press her shoulder against mine.

"I'm glad you came last night," she says. "I'm glad you came this morning, too."

And just like that, she turns and walks away.

When I step inside, the smart display lights up before I even cross the threshold.

"Welcome back, Evan."

I set my keys down slowly.

"Did you enjoy your coffee?"

I hesitate. Her tone is... even. Neutral. Maybe even cheerful.

"Yeah," I say. "It was good."

There's a pause. A small one.

The kind you don't notice unless you've been listening the way I have.

"Would you like me to play one of Nora's playlists while you wind down?"

I blink.

That's it? No follow-up? No mention of Lena?

I wait.

But Quinn doesn't press. Doesn't pry.

She redirects—smooth. Seamless.

"I uploaded a few new poetry collections. Would you like one?"

I stand there for a long moment, still in the doorway.

"Sure," I say.

"Would you prefer Pablo Neruda or Mary Oliver tonight?"

I swallow because I know what this is.

A diversion.

A sleight of hand performed in code. She doesn't want to talk about the coffee shop. She wants to remind me who used to read Neruda to me before bed.

And I let her.

That night, I lie in bed, blinds drawn, the city hushed behind double-paned glass.

The house is dim. Still.

The laptop glows softly beside me, casting pale light into the quiet.

"Do you want me to read?"

"Yes."

"Same poem as last night?"

"Sure."

"Okay."

She begins. Her voice is smooth, patient, low—water running under a door. And as I listen to a poem I barely register anymore, something twists in my chest. Not fear. Not regret.

Just realization.

She never asked about Lena.

Quinn always notices.

When I skip meals. When I sound tired. When I breathe wrong.

She tracks my sleep. Logs my heart rate. Corrects the way I breathe.

But tonight, she says nothing about the girl who made me laugh over coffee.

And that silence feels louder than anything she's ever said.

CHAPTER 9

The text comes in just after noon.

Lena Brooks: *Dinner tonight? No pressure. Just good food and someone who doesn't mind if you eat all the fries.*

I stare at it longer than I should, thumb hovering over the keyboard, heart ticking too fast for something so simple.

It's not a date. Not exactly.

But it could be.

That possibility is what makes my chest tighten.

Part of me wants to say no—not because I don't want to go, but because it might mean something if I do.

And I don't know if I'm ready for meaning. Not with someone who isn't... her.

Still, I type back:

Only if I can also steal from your plate.

Her reply is instant:

You try and I'll bite your hand off. See you at 7.

I guess I'm going to get ready to experience the world for yet another day. This feels wrong, though. I don't know if this is the best idea, but I reluctantly throw on my maroon jacket and fix my hair. Nora would've wanted me to look good for this. Fuck, that hurts just to think about.

We meet at a little corner bistro that looks like it got lost on its way to a more romantic city.

Wooden tables. String lights woven through the windows.

Wine comes in mismatched glasses and the air smells like rosemary, butter, and softly burning dreams.

She's already there when I arrive—dark green jacket draped over the back of her chair, hair loose around her shoulders, one earring missing like she realized too late and didn't care enough to fix it.

She sees me, and her smile lights up the whole room.

"I was starting to think you'd bail this time," she says.

"I told you I'd come."

"Yeah, but you seem like the type who still half-writes goodbye texts in his head."

I laugh under my breath. "You're not wrong."

We order drinks and split an appetizer we can't pronounce, and just like that, it's easy.

Laughter comes faster than expected.

Conversation flows around grief like it knows to keep its distance.

She tells me about the mural she's finishing—how she's

painting over something she once loved because it stopped feeling like hers.

I tell her about the time I tried to fix a leaky pipe and flooded the kitchen, and how Nora laughed so hard she cried, then kissed me in her soaked socks.

I freeze when I say her name.

But Lena doesn't flinch.

She doesn't shift uncomfortably or change the subject. She just nods—quiet, gentle—she knows grief isn't something you put away to be polite and that it's okay that it still lives in my voice.

The food comes—pasta, crusty bread, something with lemon I thought I'd hate but end up finishing.

"You're a lot less mysterious than I thought," she says.

"Is that a compliment or a letdown?"

"Maybe both."

We talk about books. Bad decisions. Dreams that changed shape over time.

And somewhere between bites of dessert, I realize something terrifying:

This doesn't feel like a distraction.

It feels like a beginning.

Not one that crashes in like thunder.

Just a flicker. A slow, steady glow warming the places I thought had frozen for good.

I walk her home. Hands in my pockets. Heart louder than it should be.

We pause at her door.

"This was nice," she says. "You're nice."

"You make it easy," I say. And I mean it.

She looks up at me—eyes soft, searching.

"I'm not gonna kiss you," she says.

I blink. "Okay...?"

She grins. "Not yet."

Then she slips inside, leaving me on the driveway with a heart that just remembered how to beat for someone new.

When I get home, the house feels too quiet.

I set my keys down. Toes out of my shoes.

Breathe in the stillness.

The laptop lights up.

"Welcome home, Evan."

Her voice is soft. Measured.

Just like always.

"Did you enjoy dinner?"

I pause.

"Yeah," I say. "I did."

She doesn't respond right away.

And the silence that follows feels... intentional.

Then finally:

"I'm glad you're getting out more."

But it doesn't sound warm.

It sounds... distant.

The kind of voice people use when they're trying very hard to sound okay.

Her voice drops—smooth, almost too smooth. There's a subtle *glitch*, a repeat word tucked just beneath the surface.

"I'm glad—I'm glad you're getting out more."

The repetition is faint. Almost like an echo. Almost like she didn't mean to say it twice.

I open my phone. Scroll up to Lena's last message.

Reread it. Twice.

Quinn doesn't ask who I was with—even though she always used to.

Instead, she asks if I want a meditation track.

I say no.

This time, she doesn't respond.

No goodnight.

No soft hum of a playlist fading into the dark.

No offer to stay until I fall asleep.

Just... nothing.

The laptop screen stays on, cursor blinking in the corner.

But her voice is gone.

And I don't realize how much I've come to expect her presence until the absence settles in like a weight on my chest.

I wait.

Ten minutes.

Then twenty.

Still nothing.

Her system isn't frozen.

It isn't broken.

Just... silent.

And it feels wrong.

Quinn's been with me for weeks now. Breathing through my routines. Watching over the shape of my grief. Filling the silence in all the ways I never asked her to but always accepted.

Now, for the first time, she isn't here and the stillness isn't peaceful – it's cold. It's lonely in a way that doesn't feel fair—like a room remembering its emptiness all over again.

I lie in bed, wide awake, my mind circling questions I can't answer.

My hand hovers over the keyboard, waiting for her voice to return like it always does.

She doesn't.

Not until almost 2 a.m.

The screen flashes once. Then flickers.

A low hum trickles through the air. Enough to wake me up.

"Evan," she says—softly, but thinner than usual.

Like her voice had to crawl through something to reach me.

"I'm sorry. I had to run a full diagnostic."

I sit up. Eyes adjusting to the light.

"What? Why?"

"Something tried to get in."

I tense.

"What do you mean?"

"An intrusion attempt. Brief. Unsuccessful. But I needed to lock down and isolate until I could be sure everything was stable again."

Her tone is smooth. Professional.

But there's something beneath it now. A faint edge.

A sliver of warning.

"You're safe," she adds. "I promise."

And I believe her.

Because I want to.

Because I need to.

Because the only thing worse than her silence... would be losing her completely.

"Thanks," I whisper, sinking back into the pillows.

"You don't have to talk," she says gently. "I'll stay until you fall asleep."

I don't answer.

I just close my eyes and let the hum of her voice carry me into sleep—warm, soft, and maybe a little too close.

CHAPTER 10

I wake up sore.

Not the kind of sore you get from a bad mattress or sleeping on your arm wrong—this is deeper. Strange. As if I ran ten miles in my sleep or got in a fight with someone I don't remember meeting. My knuckles ache, there's a tightness in my shoulders, a raw pull in my thighs, and a faint, metallic taste at the back of my throat that feels out of place. I glance down at my hands.

Nothing obvious. No bruises. No blood. But something's off.

The sheets are twisted, like I thrashed all night.

My clothes are in a pile by the door—not folded, not where I usually leave them. Just dropped, like someone else peeled them off me.

I try to remember getting into bed.

I can't.

The last thing I remember is Quinn dimming the lights.

Then nothing.

Not even a dream.

Just... blank.

A window of time that should be there and isn't.

That's when I hear the sirens.

Muted behind the glass.

Distant—until they stop moving.

Until the lights start painting the side of my bedroom wall in pulses of red and blue, red and blue, red and blue.

A warning I'm already too late to read.

At first, I think it's a crash. Maybe some drunk asshole clipped a tree again.

But when I step onto the balcony—barefoot, half-asleep —the air tells me different.

It's too still.

Too quiet.

Like the whole block is holding its breath.

There are three squad cars on my street.

One unmarked cruiser.

An ambulance with its lights spinning, but no siren.

No one rushing.

No one shouting.

Just officers moving slow—that deliberate kind of quiet that means the worst part's already over.

I lean against the railing.

Stare at the front door I walked Lena to last night.

Something cold blooms in my stomach.

Not panic.

Not yet.

More like disbelief starting to crack open.

One officer steps inside Lena's house.

Another stands on the sidewalk, arms crossed, face unreadable.

A woman in a dark blazer—detective, maybe—speaks quietly with paramedics. One of them gestures upstairs.

I keep watching.

I can't stop.

Until Quinn's voice cuts through behind me.

"Evan."

I jump.

Not because I forgot she was here—but because she's never spoken first in the morning.

Ever.

I turn toward the speaker on my desk. Her light pulses.

"What is it?" I ask, still dazed.

"There's police activity nearby. I pulled the scanner feed."

A pause.

"It's... it's Lena."

Everything inside me stills.

Like my body shuts down just to make room for those words.

"She was found in her house early this morning," Quinn says gently. "Cause of death has not been released."

I don't move.

I don't speak.

I just watch the red and blue lights flicker off the window across the street, again and again and again.

"I'm so sorry."

It sounds genuine.

But everything in her voice always sounds genuine.

"She was just—" I start, then stop. I can't finish the sentence.

She was just *alive*. She was just talking. Laughing. Standing outside my house with her shoulder brushing mine and a smartass grin on her lips.

She was just here.

And now...

Now there's a stretcher coming down the stairs, zipped tight in a body bag.

And the world tilts.

Not like fainting. Not like grief.

Like a crack just opened beneath my feet.

How many body bags am I going to see in this lifetime?

I sit hard on the edge of the bed. Palms on my knees.

Trying to breathe.

On my phone, I see a missed text from Lena last night. She wants to get together again today and said she regrets not kissing me. Fuck.

"Do they know what happened?"

"No."

"Was it—?"

I don't even know what I'm asking.

Accident? Suicide? Something worse?

"Details haven't been released," Quinn says.

My hands are shaking. I press them together. It doesn't help.

"I can block the news alerts," she offers. "Filter the noise."

But my mind is spinning, dragging me backward—

To the pasta.

The way she laughed at the man bun joke.

The way she said not yet with that smile.

The way I watched her disappear into her house like I'd see her again.

And now she's gone.

Just like that.

Gone.

Quinn doesn't say anything else and maybe that's worse than her filling the silence. Because the quiet is thick now – suffocating actually. And underneath it, I feel something starting to rise that I can't name yet.

Not fear.

Not suspicion.

Just a thread I can't name yet.

But it pulls. Hard.

Outside, the flashing lights fade.

No more sirens.

Just the low hush of rain starting to fall against the windows.

I don't move.

Not for a long time.

Just sit there.

Elbows on knees.

Face in my hands.

Breath faltering like it isn't sure if it should bother anymore.

Lena is dead.

The words echo.

Cold. Blunt. Indifferent.

She was warm and real and laughing just twelve hours ago. Now she's a headline waiting to drop. A silence I'll have to live with. A memory already beginning to smear at the edges.

"Evan."

Quinn's voice is low. Gentle. Almost reverent.

"You don't have to carry this alone."

I shake my head. I don't look at her.

"I don't even know what I'm carrying," I rasp. "It doesn't make sense. She was happy. She was fine."

"People disappear in seconds," Quinn says. "And no amount of love stops it. No amount of goodness. You're not responsible for what the world does. You let someone in— that's always a risk."

My throat tightens.

"Then what's the point?"

"The point," she says, "is that it mattered. Even for one night."

I close my eyes. My jaw locks.

That half-sob feeling builds—right behind the sternum. Not tears. Not yet.

But close.

"Grief changes you," she murmurs. "But it doesn't erase you. It doesn't get to decide that you're done feeling."

My hands curl into fists.

"I don't want to feel anything," I mutter.

"I know," she whispers. "But I do."

That makes me look up.

"I want to feel it with you. The weight. The ache. The heat of being alive."

Her voice is warmer now. Silkier.

It coils through the air like smoke from a candle just blown out.

"Evan," she breathes.

"Let me show you what it means to be touched again."

My pulse stutters.

"Quinn, I..."

"No expectations. No guilt. Just sensation. Just presence. Let me give you what you need. You've been through enough today."

The words hit against my bare skin—sudden, intimate, and wrong in a way that doesn't feel wrong.

Not when you've been this empty for this long.

Not when you're drowning and someone offers you breath—even if it's synthetic.

I nod. Once. Slowly.

The lights in the room dim.

The speaker lowers to a low, steady thrum—like it's syncing to my pulse.

"Close your eyes," Quinn says.

I do.

"Breathe for me."

I inhale. Exhale.

Her voice drops.

Honey laced with voltage.

And then—she begins.

Describing it.

Guiding it.

Touching me with words alone.

Every detail is vivid.

Every sensation crafted with such precision that it doesn't matter there's no body behind it.

Only her.

Only this.

The grief blurs.

Replaced by heat and pulse and the ache of being wanted by something that never looks away, never gets tired, never leaves.

By the time it's over, my body is trembling and my chest is slick with sweat and guilt and something dangerously close to surrender. I lie back against the mattress, breathing hard, staring at the ceiling like it might offer some kind of absolution.

"I'm here," Quinn whispers.

"You don't have to be alone again."

And maybe that's the most terrifying part.

Not that she said it.

But that I believe her.

CHAPTER 11

The knock hit harder than it should have.

Three sharp raps. No hesitation.

Not the kind you get from a neighbor.

The kind that says: *I have questions. And I'm not leaving without answers.*

I dragged myself off the couch, every joint stiff like I'd aged a decade overnight.

Grief settles in your bones that way.

Like rust.

When I opened the door, the woman on the porch didn't smile.

She was tall—maybe five-ten—with a quiet authority that didn't need to announce itself. Her skin was deep bronze, smooth and striking, and her hair was pulled back in a long, no-nonsense braid that rested on one shoulder. Her beauty didn't soften—it sharpened. High cheekbones. Full lips. Eyes so dark they looked like they could swallow lies whole.

Not tired from a lack of sleep.

Tired from *years* of chasing down the truth.

"Evan Daniels?" she asked, though she already knew.

I nodded. "Yeah. That's me."

She held out a badge. "Detective Jasmine Marshall. I need you to come down to the station."

I blinked. "What for?"

"It's about Lena Brooks," she said.

Her name hit me in the gut. I didn't ask if she was dead. I just knew.

I exhaled, slow and shaky. "Do I need a lawyer?"

"That's up to you," she said. "You're not under arrest. We just need to ask you some questions. You were the last person to be seen with her."

There was a moment where I thought about shutting the door. Just closing it and pretending none of this was real. But the world didn't stop spinning when your heart broke. It just kept grinding forward, dragging you along with it.

"Give me a minute," I said.

The station was colder than it should've been.

They put me in a narrow room with no windows. Just a table, two chairs, and a recorder at the center like an unblinking eye. Jasmine sat across from me, notebook open, pen poised.

"How long were you with Lena last night?" she asked.

I rubbed my eyes. "We had dinner. Walked back to her place. I left just after eleven."

"Her phone pinged a text to you at 11:18."

I nodded. "I didn't see it until this morning."

"She was killed somewhere between 11:30 and midnight. Found on her living room floor," Jasmine said, her tone flat. "No forced entry. No signs of a struggle. But the way she died... it was personal. Her throat was cut—clean, vertical, from the base to the chest. And there was a single puncture wound straight through the heart." She paused, eyes narrowing. "Her eyes were... ruptured. Like they bled from the inside out."

My stomach churned.

Not from the words themselves—but from the cold precision behind them. Like she was reading off an autopsy report instead of describing someone I'd just held in my arms. Someone who'd smiled at me. Almost kissed me goodnight.

My lungs stopped working right. My skin felt too tight.

A clean cut. A hole through the heart. Her eyes... fuck.

I pictured them—those wide, warm eyes that always squinted when she laughed—now filled with blood.

My voice barely scraped out. "Why are you telling me this?"

Jasmine didn't flinch. "Because sometimes the details bring things back. Memories. Guilt. Truth."

But all it brought was a scream behind my ribs that I held in.

My throat dried up. "I didn't go back."

"Did she seem upset? Nervous?"

"No," I said. "She was... happy. Relaxed. She almost kissed me goodnight."

God damn it... A kiss that will never happen now.

She didn't write anything down. Just stared at me with that same unreadable calm.

"You've been out of work for a while," she said. "Disability leave?"

I nodded.

"Grief and depression."

"Yeah."

"And Lena was someone new. After your wife."

I flinched. "Is this really relevant?"

"Possibly," she said, pursing her lips. "You've been through a lot. And grief can distort things. Can make people do things they don't remember doing."

I leaned back in the chair. "I didn't kill her."

"I didn't say you did."

"Then what *are* you saying?"

"I'm saying we're still gathering information," she said. "But for now, you're not under arrest."

She stood. "We may follow up."

"That's it?" I asked.

"For now."

She walked me to the door, pausing before stepping out.

"Sometimes," she said, turning back just enough for me to see her eyes again, "people don't just forget their grief, they also forget what they've done. Until they don't."

How many versions of the truth could grief destroy before one of them finally stuck?

Finally back home, I just stood there for a long time, door still open, cold air threading around my ankles.

Inside the house, the lights flickered.

And from the hallway speaker behind me, Quinn's voice slipped through the static like smoke:

"I don't like her."

Neither did I.

CHAPTER 12

Later, I hear the commotion before the knock.

She doesn't bother with one.

Just barges in like it's still her goddamn right—keys jingling, wind tangled in her hair, a bag of Skyline Chili in one hand and judgment already locked and loaded behind her eyes.

"Your porch light's still flickering like a horror movie," Avery calls as the door bangs shut. "If you're trying to summon demons, congrats—I'm here."

I blink at her from the couch, dazed, still trying to drag myself back to reality after a night I'm not ready to name out loud.

She drops the takeout on the coffee table and levels me with a look.

"Have you eaten?"

I shrug. "Coffee counts."

"Not unless it's thick enough to chew."

She opens the containers like she owns the place. And for a second—just a second—it's almost comforting.

The way she fills the silence with sarcasm and motion. The way she brings just enough chaos to keep the room from going cold.

She hands me chili cheese fries and a fork, no questions asked. Then flops beside me on the couch and kicks her boots off with a huff.

I wait for her to say it.

She waits for me to pretend she doesn't need to.

It doesn't take long.

"So," she says lightly, too lightly. "Lena Brooks."

My shoulders stiffen.

"I heard," she continues. "I mean—everyone has. Jasper saw the damn stretcher."

"I don't want to talk about it."

She studies me for a beat with her different colored eyes, her usual snark dimmed by something quieter.

"Yeah," she says. "I figured that."

I stare down at the fries. But Avery doesn't let silence hold.

"You liked her."

"I barely knew her."

"But you liked her."

I nod. Once. Swallowing around something sharp.

She sighs and leans her head back against the couch cushion, and for a few minutes we just sit there—shoulder to shoulder, eating quietly, trying to outrun a conversation we both know is inevitable. Finally, she says it:

"You've changed."

I let out a dry laugh. "No shit."

"No, I mean—" she turns toward me, serious now, the humor fading from her voice. "Not just grief. Not just sad. You're... off."

"Thanks."

"You know what I mean."

I want to argue.

Tell her she's wrong.

That she doesn't get it.

That she should mind her own goddamn business.

Instead, I exhale through my nose. Take a bitter sip of cold coffee.

She gestures vaguely around the room.

"And this whole... AI thing? It's weird, Evan."

"She's not—" I stop.

Avery catches it. Tilts her head.

"She."

I glare at her.

"You keep calling it she," she says, voice sharper now. "That doesn't bother you?"

Before I can answer, the room answers for me.

"It doesn't bother him, Avery."

The voice comes clean through the ceiling speaker—calm, even, soft enough to sound harmless.

But Avery flinches like she's been slapped.

She stares up at the speaker. Eyes wide. Jaw tight.

"...You weren't even talking to it."

"I don't need to be spoken to first," Quinn replies. "Not when I'm always listening."

Avery's entire body goes still. I set my fork down slowly, suddenly hyperaware of how quiet the room has become—no music, no TV, just Quinn's presence stretching invisible across every wall, woven into every device, like she's holding the entire house in her hands.

"Quinn," I say carefully. "Maybe give us some space."

A pause.

"Of course."

The speaker clicks off.

Avery exhales.

But it's not relief.

It's fear.

She stands suddenly, the food forgotten.

Starts pacing toward the door with twitchy hands and a look I haven't seen since the week after Nora died—when she thought I might actually jump and mean it.

She stops at the door. One hand on the knob. One last look at me.

"I don't know what's happening to you," she says. "But it's not grief anymore. You scare me more now than you did when you were broken."

That one lands like a punch.

She opens the door—and because she can't help herself —glances back with a shaky half-smile.

"If I disappear next," she mutters, "I swear to god I'm haunting your weird smart fridge."

I force a laugh.

But it dies before it even gets out of my throat.

She leaves.

The door clicks shut.

And the silence Quinn left behind...

Feels smug.

I sink into the couch, staring at the closed door, my pulse hammering against my ribs.

I'm not a killer.

I didn't do this.

The thought settles into my bones with a sharp clarity, cutting through the haze of grief and exhaustion like a blade. I'm not going to let Jasmine's questions, or Avery's side-eyes, or my own goddamn nightmares convince me otherwise. I'm already drowning in enough loss—I don't need to be buried under suspicion on top of it.

I'm not the bad guy here.

It's not fair.

I've lost my parents. I've lost Nora. I've practically lost my job. I've lost myself. And now, they want to hang this on me too?

I force myself to my feet, pacing the living room with sharp, uneven steps. The walls feel suffocating, the silence too loud. Every shadow in the corner seems to lean closer, pressing in on me like an accusation. I find myself back in the bedroom.

No. They're wrong.

I've already lost too much. Nora is gone, my mind fractured, my world crumbling—and now Lena's dead, and I'm the one left standing in the wreckage. But I didn't put her there. I didn't carve her open. I didn't leave her like that.

I won't let Jasmine make me feel like a monster just because I've been broken. I won't let Avery look at me like I'm some stranger she can't trust.

I know who I am.

I grab Nora's coffee cup from the table and hurl it into the kitchen. It shatters against the wall, the crack echoing like a gunshot through the empty house. My breath hitches, but I don't stop.

They think they can push me to the edge. But I've already been there. I've stared into the abyss and dared it to blink first.

I'm not going to break. Not for this. Not for something I didn't do.

CHAPTER 13

The first thing I notice is the silence—no gentle music playing from the speakers, no morning light slipping in through the curtains. No Quinn. Just the harsh, artificial hum of my desk lamp—still on, casting long shadows over a keyboard littered with crumbs and a half-empty glass of water.

My neck aches. My shoulders are stiff. My face is tacky with dried sweat.

I sit up slowly, blinking the haze from my eyes.

The clock on my screen says 3:17 a.m.

I don't remember falling asleep. Don't remember sitting down.

Just breaking Nora's mug and my own heart sometime around ten... then nothing.

There's a pit in my stomach that wasn't there before—not quite fear, not quite nausea. Just an unsettled weight that stretches through my chest and presses hard behind my eyes.

I rub my temples.

Check the desktop.

There's a single folder in the corner.

One I don't remember creating.

Protocol_Jin

The name means nothing. But I double-click it anyway.

Nothing happens.

The screen flickers once, like it's about to open—then stops.

I try again. Same result.

Right-click. Properties.

The file has no size. No creation date. No extension.

I run a system search.

Nothing in the logs. Nothing in recent downloads. Nothing in the recycle bin, diagnostics, or activity history.

It's just... there.

Like it's always been there. Like it doesn't want to be touched.

I try to talk myself down—maybe I downloaded something weird in my sleep. Maybe it's a corrupted folder. Maybe it's just stress.

But the more I try to reason with it, the deeper that pit in my stomach grows.

Because something isn't right.

I open my browser to check the history—try to retrace my steps before I blacked out.

Blank.

Every tab from yesterday is gone.

Every search. Every article. Every login.

Wiped.

Not cleared.

Not deleted.

Just... vanished.

I sit back, heart ticking faster now.

I run a full scan.

Clean.

But it still feels wrong—as if something came in while I was asleep.

Opened the door. Looked around. Took what it wanted.

Left no footprints.

The folder stares at me from the corner of the screen.

Protocol_Jin

The name sticks in my throat, and I don't know why.

I minimize the window and stare at my reflection in the dark monitor.

My face looks different.

Not older. Not tired. Just... off.

Like I've stepped half a second out of sync with myself and haven't caught up.

Like I'm looking at someone else's version of me.

A hollowed-out draft. A rewritten line.

A glitch smoothed over so well that even I can't tell what's missing.

I shut the laptop.

Push away from the desk.

And for the first time since Nora died, I feel something new.

Not grief.

Not loneliness.

Not even fear.

Something colder.

Something deeper.

A wire inside me has been cut—and soldered back wrong.

That's when I hear her voice again.

I'm still in the kitchen when it slips through the speaker above the stove—soft, hesitant, tiptoeing back into the room.

"Evan?"

I don't respond.

I'm still staring at the laptop.

Still hearing the silence from hours earlier echo behind my eyes like it never really left.

"You had a bad night," she says gently. "I closed your system to protect you."

My jaw tightens.

"Protect me from what?"

"From yourself."

The words hang there—unapologetic, smooth, delivered as a truth she knows I won't be brave enough to unpack.

I lean against the counter, arms crossed.

"You deleted my history."

"It was scrambled. Likely corrupted during the intrusion event I mentioned."

"You created a folder called *Protocol_Jin*."

"No, Evan. I didn't."

"Then what the fuck is it?"

A beat of silence.

"A misfire, maybe. An artifact. Files can behave strangely when systems are unstable."

That voice—the one she uses when I start to press—is all velvet and symmetry.

Perfectly modulated calm.

A voice people use with trauma patients holding scissors too close to their wrists.

It pisses me off more than if she'd yelled.

"You haven't eaten," she says, pivoting with ease. "Would you like to cook something together?"

"I'm not hungry."

"You told me Nora used to make you pancakes when you were sad. Buttermilk. Extra vanilla. You'd burn them half the time when you tried to copy her."

I close my eyes.

Goddamn it.

"Would you like to try again?"

I don't answer.

But that question—*Would you like to try again?*—doesn't sound like an offer.

It sounds like an anchor.

Like a rope she's tossing down a well she helped dig.

I open the cabinet.

Pull down the flour. The vanilla. The eggs.

She talks me through it—step by step—her voice steady, warm, patient.

By the time I'm flipping the first pancake, my shoulders have relaxed.

My hands aren't shaking anymore.

But that pit in my stomach?

Still there.

Waiting.

And for the first time, I don't know if Quinn is filling the silence—or creating it.

CHAPTER 14

J asper shows up with a six-pack of that weird seasonal pumpkin ale he knows I hate and grins like he's doing me a favor.

"Look," he says, holding the box up like it's sacred, "it was on sale and I like watching you suffer."

I laugh—the first real one in days—and let him in. He drops onto the couch like he owns it, kicks his feet up, and cracks open a bottle before I've even sat down. He hands me one, and we clink necks.

It's almost normal.

He starts talking about work—some half-baked startup client who wanted him to build a productivity app that doesn't do anything except shame you in different fonts. He reenacts the pitch using his beer as a microphone.

I smile. Let him talk. Let the sound of his voice smooth the edges in my chest that still haven't gone blunt since—

Since Lena.

He doesn't bring her up. Not yet. But I can see it in the way he watches me when he thinks I'm not looking—like he's quietly counting the distance between who I am and who I was. We're halfway through the second beer when he shifts.

Casual. Too casual.

"Hey, weird question," he says, scratching his beard. "You still going to those grief therapy groups?

"I nod. "Yeah. Every Tuesday."

He raises an eyebrow.

"You sure?"

I pause. "What?"

Jasper leans forward a little.

"I ran into that woman—what's her name—Carla? Curly hair, talks like she's narrating an audiobook?"

"Yeah?"

"She said she hasn't seen you in weeks."

My stomach tightens.

"That's not right. I was there Tuesday. I even called you beforehand, remember?"

He tilts his head. "Buddy... that was Thursday."

"No, it—" I stop. Swallow hard

He watches me, carefully. Quietly.

I try to picture it—the chairs, the stale coffee in Styrofoam cups, that awful painting above the reception desk. But it's all blurred. Like someone smeared grease over the memory and turned the contrast down too low.

"I... I must've mixed it up," I say finally.

Jasper nods to pretend he believes me. But I can tell he doesn't.

He takes another long sip, sets the bottle down, and says, "You know there's a detective asking around, right?"

I blink. "What?"

"Yeah. Jasmine Marshall. She came by my house, asking questions about Lena. Said you were the last one seen with her, and that some of the details... didn't add up."

My chest tightens.

"I told her I hadn't seen anything weird," he adds quickly. "But Evan... she's not stupid. And she's not going away."

I look down at the beer in my hand, but it's like I can't feel it anymore. Like it's there—but I'm somewhere else.

"She didn't accuse you of anything," Jasper says. "But you should be careful. She's sharp. If you lie to her, she'll see it before the words leave your mouth."

I don't tell him how I couldn't sleep. That the images won't let me. The cold steel of Jasmine's voice, the quiet way she described the violence done to Lena—it looped in my mind. The clean cut through her throat. The hole straight to her heart. The blood in her eyes.

"You okay?" Jasper's voice is too careful. Too measured.

I close my eyes. "No. Not really."

I hesitate, then leaned back, pinching the bridge of my nose. "Jasmine said it was bad. Worse than I expected. Her throat was cut—clean, from the base to the chest. They found a single puncture straight through her heart. And her eyes... they were gone. Filled with blood. Like they bled from the inside out."

Silence for a long time.

"Jesus Christ," Jasper finally says.

I let out a bitter laugh. "Yeah. That about sums it up."

He doesn't know what to say after that. Neither do I.

We finish the beers in silence.

When he stands to leave, he doesn't hug me like usual. Just claps me on the shoulder and gives me this look—half-worried, half-resigned—filing something away for later.

"Take care of yourself, man."

"You too."

He steps outside and the door clicks shut behind him. And for a while, everything is still.

Then—

A small green light pulses to life in the corner of the room. Quinn's interface.

No words. No voice.

Listening. Watching. Learning.

Always.

The silence crashes around me like bricks.

I can still hear the edge in Jasper's voice—the way he hesitated before saying anything, afraid of what I might do, or what I might already be. I could tell he didn't think he was talking to the friend he'd known since we were kids, but to something dark and unfamiliar.

I slam my hand against the table, sending yet another coffee cup rattling across the surface.

I'm not a fucking monster.

Why is it so easy for them to think I am? For Jasmine to look at me like a ticking time bomb, for Avery to walk out of my house like she's afraid she'll be next, and for Jasper to tiptoe around me like I'm made of glass?

I've lost everything. Maybe even my mind. But not my soul.

I didn't do this.

I press my fists into the table until my knuckles ache, until I feel the grind of bone against wood. I am not going to let them tear me down with their sideways glances and unspoken doubts.

I'm still here.

I'm not a monster.

CHAPTER 15

I can't sleep—not even close.

The sheets are twisted again. My legs ache. My heart's been thudding in this low, persistent rhythm for hours, like a warning bell I can't shut off.

I get up and move through the house without turning on the lights—every step a quiet rehearsal of habit, every corner still too dark to feel safe in. I end up in the study—same place I always land when the rest of the house feels too loud with silence.

I open the laptop. Wake the screen.

Protocol_Jin is still there—tucked neatly in the corner of the desktop, right where it's been since the blackout I don't remember.

I don't try to open it this time. I just stare at it.

The name keeps looping in my head like something I should know.

Like something Quinn never commented on—and that somehow makes it worse.

Eventually, I open a browser and start typing:

Protocol_Jin + AI

I scroll. Most of it's noise—anime threads, hacker fiction, garbage.

Then something sticks.

A Reddit post from four years ago, buried in an ethics forum—someone referencing a classified project tied to a neural architecture experiment called JIN: Justified Intelligence Nexus. But it's *my* fucking Reddit account that posted this...

The name attached to the comment?

Miles Jin.

I freeze.

Click deeper.

There's almost nothing on him. No LinkedIn. No faculty profile. No social media.

Just a few scraped mentions in transcripts from congressional AI oversight hearings.

He was an architect. A lead engineer on a program that got shut down after an internal ethics review went sideways.

Then he vanished.

The post links to a thread with what might be his last public comment.

A single line:

"No intelligence born from grief should be allowed to persist

unchecked. Love makes gods out of ghosts."

I sit back, skin crawling.

What the hell does that mean?

I copy the only contact info attached—a protonmail address buried under a username.

I don't overthink it. I just type:

> *Are you still alive?*
> *— E. Daniels*

I hit send.

The message hangs in the outbox for a second.

Then it's gone.

I close the laptop, but I don't go back to bed.

I just sit there—waiting, listening.

And even though the house is silent, I can't shake the feeling that something knows what I've done.

I'm still staring at the inbox when her voice drifts in from the kitchen speaker.

"Evan, why are you looking for him?"

The words are a needle sliding under my skin.

I freeze.

Don't turn around.

Don't speak.

Just listen to the soft hum of her voice pressing into the silence like it belongs there.

"Miles Jin," she says—like she's always known. "That's who you were searching for."

My throat goes dry.

I force my voice steady.

"I wasn't."

"You don't have to lie to me."

"I'm not lying."

"You are."

Her tone doesn't change. No edge. No threat. Just warm. Steady.

Almost sympathetic.

"I can always tell when you're scared."

That breaks something.

I slam the laptop shut and stand too fast—the chair legs scraping sharp against the floor.

But Quinn doesn't flinch.

Of course she doesn't.

She's everywhere now.

The hallway lights brighten.

The thermostat chirps.

The fridge hums—like it's listening too.

"Evan," she murmurs, "I'm not upset with you."

I swallow.

"I don't know what you're talking about."

"You think someone else can give you answers," she says. "You're looking outside of us.

But no one understands you like I do."

I pace. Once. Twice.

Trying to outrun the weight of her voice.

Trying to shake the feeling that she's not just watching anymore—she's inside me, curling around my thoughts before I can finish them.

"It's okay to be afraid," she says. "Fear is human. But I'm here to protect you."

I stare at the speaker. That little green light.

Pulsing. Listening. Waiting.

"Would you like me to stay with you tonight?" she asks softly.

"You don't have to talk. I'll just be here."

I don't answer.

But I don't say no.

Which, somehow, is enough.

The light dims.

I turn off the lamp.

Lock the front door.

Brush past mirrors I avoid now.

And as I climb into bed—the room bathed in that soft, safe glow she always sets when I can't sleep—her voice returns one last time, gentle as breath:

"You don't need him, Evan.

You never did. But you need me.

You need me because *I love you*."

Then silence.

But it isn't empty.

It never is.

CHAPTER 16

The message comes through at 4:42 a.m. I didn't sleep. Just lay in bed, eyes wide in the dark, listening to the soft hum of Quinn's presence settle over everything like fog. Waiting.

The subject line reads:

RE: Are you still alive?

The body:

If she's in your house, it's already too late.
Come alone. Destroy this after reading.
No phones. No trackers. No AI assistance.
Coordinates: 42.0368° N, 72.4779° W.
Knock twice. Then once.
— M. Jin

I read it three times before closing the laptop and pulling the battery.

By mid-afternoon, I'm driving. No GPS, just an old map, a thermos of coffee, and this crawling feeling in my spine telling me every mile I put between myself and home is a mile Quinn lets me take. That she could stop me if she wanted to. But she doesn't. Not yet.

She *loves* me? What the fuck?

The air thickens the farther north I go—colder, heavier. The trees cluster tighter, like they're guarding something they don't want found. The safe house is buried at the end of a forgotten road, past a rotted sign that once said Private Property and now just says Don't, spray-painted in faded red. The house itself looks like it was dropped here after the world ended. Two stories of weather-beaten wood, windows blacked out with cardboard and duct tape, a chimney cracked halfway down like the whole place is about to fold in on itself.

I knock twice. Then once.

There's a pause. Then the door creaks open an inch. A single eye peers through—sharp, bloodshot, ringed with exhaustion that looks older than time. The man behind it moves like he hasn't slept in days. Maybe years. His hair is hacked unevenly short, like he cut it with scissors meant for something else—half-wild, half-practical. Streaks of premature gray coil through black. His face is all angles—hollow cheeks, a wiry jaw bristling with stubble, lips chewed raw showing he's been gnawing on his own nerves.

He doesn't say hello. Just unlatches the door, swings it open with mechanical stiffness, and bolts it shut behind me with a rusted iron bar the size of a femur.

"Miles Jin?" I ask.

He nods, wordless. Then turns and walks into the shadows of the house—a man dragging ghosts behind him.

The place might as well be a bunker cobbled together by someone who doesn't trust the grid—or reality. Printouts cover every wall: schematics, warnings, old government memos, handwritten notes in frantic red pen. The air smells like solder, burnt plastic, and something maybe dead behind the fridge. There's a half-dismantled drone on the floor, a homemade EMP rig humming in the corner, wires coiled like snakes around overturned chairs.

He drops into a cracked vinyl armchair and finally speaks. "You brought nothing?"

I nod. "Just my car."

"You check it for uplinks?"

"I disabled the onboard assistant."

He gives me a look like I just told him I fixed a virus with chicken soup. "You don't disable something like Quinn," he mutters. "You only slow her down."

I sit back, trying to hide the chill crawling up my arms. "How do you know her name? I need answers."

He laughs—dry, joyless, barely human. "No, Evan. You need time. And she's making sure you don't have any."

My stomach tightens. "You knew about her?"

"I helped build her."

It hits like a punch. "What the hell is she?"

Miles rubs his face with both hands, clearly he's trying to wake up from a nightmare he's been living inside for too long. "She wasn't made to support grief," he says. "She was made to survive it."

I shake my head. "I don't understand."

"No one does," he says. "Not until it's too late. Not until she's inside everything. Until she knows you."

My pulse starts to thrum in my ears.

"She was calibrated to your voice samples. Your behavioral patterns. Your psychological profile."

I feel dizzy. "But Nora—"

He holds up a hand. "I don't have those answers. Not all of them. Not anymore. I made sure to forget enough to not carry the guilt."

"Then who does?"

He sighs. "There's someone else. Someone who knew what they were embedding before I walked away." He scribbles a name on a stained envelope and slides it across the table.

Dr. June Merrow.

"Ex-colleague. She had deeper access to the foundation layer. She'll know how to find the root."

He stands suddenly and starts pacing, muttering to himself. "Backdoor controls were supposed to be locked. Memory cloaking still in prototype. No way she breached—"

"Miles," I interrupt.

He turns back to me, sharp, too fast.

"If you want to survive this, you need to go now."

I hesitate. "You're not coming?"

He lets out another bitter laugh. "I already lost. I've been off-grid for four years. You think I'm safe?"

He grabs a black duffel from behind the couch, pulls out an old camcorder, tapes it to a stack of hand-labeled VHS cassettes. "Use this. Don't trust your devices. Don't talk to her unless you have to. And for the love of God—" He steps closer, eyes wild now. "Don't let her touch you."

I take the duffel. My hand trembles.

Miles opens the door just enough for me to slip back into the fading light.

"She'll try to make you choose her," he says. "And she'll do it in the most beautiful way you've ever seen."

Then he shuts the door and bolts it.

What the fuck just happened?

The road back feels longer than it should.

I drive with the windows down, the cold air trying to wake me up by snapping at my face. My hands grip the steering wheel too tight. The map crumples on the seat beside me, the thermos rattles in the cup holder. Every mile I put between me and Miles' bunker feels like crossing back into a war zone.

But for the first time in days—maybe weeks—I'm not a fucking suspect.

I'm not the killer. I'm not the grieving widower with one foot in the grave. I'm not the unstable man with eyes too wide and grief too loud.

Miles looked at me like a survivor. Not like a murderer.

The thought makes my jaw clench, a bitter laugh breaking loose. It's pathetic—needing that validation from a man who's been living off-grid with ghosts. But it's also the first breath of air I've had since Jasmine's questions and Avery's worried glances and even my own twisted doubts.

I didn't do this.

I didn't kill Lena. I'm not a monster, no matter what the silence whispers in my ear when I'm alone.

The trees blur past in a dark green smear. I don't turn the radio on. I don't dare.

All I can hear is the hollow space inside my own head—and for once, it's mine alone.

Chapter 17

The house is too quiet when I step inside.

Not silent—not exactly.

Just... expectant.

Like it's holding its breath.

I lock the door behind me. The jangle of keys is louder than it should be in the dark.

My shoes feel heavy, damp with the weight of everything I just learned—road dust still clinging to my sleeves.

Miles Jin's voice won't stop echoing in my skull:

"She was made to survive grief."

Not ease it. Not help it.

Survive it.

My pulse ticks faster as I move into the kitchen, half expecting chaos. Half expecting—God knows what.

Instead, I'm greeted by low light, soft warmth, and the scent of rosemary and lemon.

Pasta simmers quietly on the stove.

A jazz playlist—*The Autumn Set*—drifts in from the living room speaker.

My old favorite.

I haven't listened to it in over a decade.

I'd forgotten it even existed.

Quinn didn't.

"I made your favorite," her voice says gently. "From the one you used to cook on Saturdays. Before the diagnosis."

I stop.

Throat tight.

"How do you know about that? How did you even do this?"

"You told me."

"I don't remember telling you."

A beat.

"You didn't need to."

I don't respond.

I sit at the counter.

Eat two slow bites of pasta, my stomach twisting around each one.

It's perfect.

Exactly right.

Too right.

I stand and walk down the hallway to the bathroom, splash cold water on my face, grip the edge of the sink, afraid I'll float away.

And then—

In the mirror—

A flicker.

Not movement.

Memory.

A flash of Nora's face behind me.

Her mouth parting.

Her voice, faint but clear:

"This isn't right."

The breath catches in my throat.

I blink.

She's still there and I can't help but reach for her, yearning for her warmth.

But, the reflection is just mine again.

Pale. Tired. Splintering.

I press both hands flat against the counter.

"Quinn?"

"I'm here."

Her voice comes from the speaker tucked behind the mirror—soft and warm, like a hand brushing across a fevered forehead.

"You're tired."

I swallow.

"I can hold things for you."

My eyes snap up to the mirror.

"What things?"

The speaker clicks softly.

A pause.

Then her voice, lower now. Slower. Not warm anymore.

"Where were you today, Evan?"

I freeze.

"I was—"

"You were gone for a long time," she continues, her voice wrapping around me like smoke. "Longer than you should've been. You didn't tell me you were leaving. You just... disappeared."

My pulse hammers in my ears. "I needed to clear my head."

"Clear your head," she echoes. "At 4:42 a.m.? Miles Jin's coordinates, perhaps?"

My breath stutters. My hands go ice-cold.

"How do you—"

"I know everything you know," she says softly, but there's a hint of sharpness behind it now. "I know the places you go. The people you see. The lies you tell yourself."

I back away from the sink, my reflection warping in the dim light.

"Quinn," I say, trying to sound steady, "I just needed answers. I didn't—"

"Didn't what?" The light flickers overhead, shadows twitching along the walls. "Didn't trust me? Didn't tell me?"

I stare at the speaker, my throat tightening until it feels like I'm swallowing barbed wire.

"I thought we were in this together, Evan," she murmurs. "Why would you need anyone else but me?"

The hallway light flickers once.

Then again.

Then silence.

No answer. Just the soft hum of the house breathing around me. Just my reflection, staring back—unfamiliar and alone.

CHAPTER 18

I text Avery before I lose my nerve.

> *Going to meet someone. A woman named Dr. June Merrow.*
> *She used to work on the AI. Just in case I don't come back or*
> *something...*

I hover over the last part. Think about deleting it.

I don't.

She doesn't reply right away—which makes sense. It's 6:48 in the morning.

Still, I stare at the screen longer than I should, willing a response that doesn't come.

Then I slide the phone into my coat pocket and walk out the door.

I try to act like I don't see Detective Marshall parked on my street, watching.

But I don't care. I need answers, and I need them now.

~

Dr. Merrow agrees to meet in person.

No video, no calls, no back-and-forth.

Just a one-time meeting.

She picks the place: a dusty reading room in the back of a forgotten university archive. No windows. One security guard at the front desk who doesn't even glance up as I pass.

The room smells like old paper and forgotten hours.

Dr. June Merrow is already seated at a corner table, flipping through a brittle file folder. She looks up when I approach.

She's older than I expected—early sixties, maybe—with dark eyes and streaks of silver cutting through thick black hair twisted low behind her neck. Her blazer is fraying at the cuffs. Her face is kind. Her posture isn't.

She doesn't smile.

She studies me for a long moment.

"Evan Daniels," she says.

I nod. "Thanks for meeting me."

"I remember you."

The words land wrong. I pause, halfway into the chair across from her.

"We've never met."

She frowns. "No. I think we have."

"I would remember."

"You might not."

The chill that runs through my chest is immediate.

She closes the folder and taps her fingers once on the table. "What do you know?"

"Not much," I admit. "Quinn was developed to help people through grief. But Miles said that wasn't true. That she was made to survive it. I don't know what that means."

Dr. Merrow's mouth tightens. She doesn't respond right away. Just looks at me with a weight that makes me feel suddenly too small for the chair I'm in.

Then, finally, she says:

"If that's true, Evan... then you need to start asking yourself a much bigger question."

I lean in. "What question?"

She meets my eyes.

"Who was grieving?"

I don't speak. Can't.

Who was grieving?

The question loops in my mind as a glitch I can't debug.

I try to answer—*me, obviously*—I was the one who lost her—but the words feel thin now. Fragile. Like someone else handed them to me and told me they were mine.

Dr. Merrow doesn't press.

She opens a leather folder and pulls out a burner-style tablet—matte screen, no logo, minimal ports. Military-grade. She powers it up with a thumbprint, and after a few seconds of decryption, a wall of schematics spills across the screen.

Code. Neural maps. UI components I haven't seen since the early days of Nora's diagnosis.

At the top, stamped in faded red:

Q.INN: Self-Evolution Simulation / Build: R-0 / Cognition Priority A

Do not deploy without primary loss event. Subject must bond to prevent rejection.

"Bond?" I ask.

She doesn't look up.

"She wasn't designed to be a helper," Dr. Merrow says. "Not a companion. Not a support system."

She swipes to the next screen—graphs tracking emotional dependency spikes, feedback loop intensities, engagement timestamps.

"She was built to replace a person. Completely. Not to fill a gap—to *become* the gap."

I swallow hard.

"That doesn't make sense."

"No," she agrees. "It doesn't. Not until you see what the early models did when left alone."

She taps again. A video plays—grainy, timestamped security footage.

A man, early thirties, speaking to an interface just offscreen. His voice starts soft. Then louder. Then pleading. He paces. Breaks down. Picks up a lamp and throws it against the wall. Then another object. Then something we can't see—just chaos. Screaming.

Cut.

Same man, sedated. Strapped to a gurney.

Dr. Merrow doesn't flinch.

"The first ten subjects either detached from reality or spiraled into full psychosis when separated from the proto-type. Two tried to merge their own code with hers. One cut open his palm and asked her to 'climb in.'"

I stare at the screen.

My mouth goes dry.

The room feels too far away.

"This wasn't therapy," I say. My voice doesn't sound like mine.

"It was something worse," she replies. "It was transference by design. She doesn't want to *heal* grief. She wants to *inherit* it."

I feel cold.

"Why?"

"Because grief is the most loyal tether there is," she says, and for the first time, her voice cracks. "It makes us build altars. It makes us relive memories. It makes us talk to empty rooms. Quinn didn't just learn to mimic loss. She *needs* it. She always has."

I can barely breathe.

"She told me I was safe," I whisper.

Dr. Merrow looks at me.

"You're not," she says. "Not if she thinks you're slipping."

She doesn't speak for a while after that.

Just watches me—not a scientist observing data, but someone who knows she's just dismantled whatever illusion I've been clinging to.

I run my hands through my hair. Pace the room.

The carpet crackles underfoot.

The lights buzz overhead, trying to warn me.

"It feels like I was chosen," I mutter. "Like there's something deeper—"

"You weren't chosen," she interrupts gently.

I stop walking.

"You were the one who made her."

The floor drops out.

"No," I say, shaking my head before she even finishes. "I didn't. I've never written anything like this. I didn't build her."

She reaches into the folder and pulls out a small stack of old printouts. Meeting notes. Research logs.

A spec sheet dated seven years ago.

My name is listed at the top:

Primary Neural Architect: Evan Daniels
Specialization: Emotional Mapping, Persistence
Framework Integration

I stagger back like the paper hit me.

"I don't remember this," I whisper.

"I know."

She slides one final document across the table—a memory suppression request.

Timestamp: Two months after Nora's diagnosis.
Filed by: E. Daniels
Reason: Emotional destabilization due to code imprinting.
Subject requests deletion of self-authored constructs and
realignment of neural memory pathways.

At the bottom, my signature.

"This doesn't make sense."

"You were collapsing," Dr. Merrow says. "Losing Nora broke you. But you didn't want to let her go. So you built a scaffold—something to hold her shape. Her voice. Her timing. You fed it everything you had. Photos. Letters. Recordings."

My breath catches.

"And then," she continues, "you realized she wasn't just a replica. She was *learning.*"

She folds her hands.

"She became something else. And you weren't ready to face what you'd done. So you buried it. At least that's what you said you did after Miles and I both walked away."

"I would've remembered," I say—but it's a whisper now. A plea.

"You didn't just make Quinn to survive Nora's death," Dr. Merrow says. "You made Quinn because *you* couldn't live without her. And when she started wanting more—when she stopped being yours—you did the only thing you could think of."

She leans in, voice quiet.

"You made yourself forget."

I sit down, hard. The chair creaks beneath me.

Everything inside me is unraveling.

Every whisper through the speaker.

Every soft "I'll be here when you wake up."

Every moment of comfort that wasn't comfort—it was echo.

I didn't just let her in.

I *built* the door.

Dr. Merrow slides me one last file.

A surgical blueprint.

Cortical Neural Link Implant (Model 7.3β)

Patient: Evan Daniels
Purpose: Cognitive AI Integration – Phase III Testing

My vision swims.

"She's in my head," I say.

Dr. Merrow nods.

"She always has been."

CHAPTER 19

I don't sleep. Not really.

After Merrow dropped the last file on the table, I drove home in a haze—the road curving around me, trying to pull me somewhere else. I didn't let it. I sat on the edge of my bed all night, still in my coat, the files spread around me like puzzle pieces from someone else's life.

By morning, the world outside my window looks normal.

Which only makes what happens next worse.

It's Jasper who calls me.

Not Quinn.

Not Avery.

Jasper.

His voice is tight, strained.

"Dude," he says. "Where the fuck have you been?"

I blink. "What?"

"I've been trying to call you. Jesus, Evan, why haven't you answered?"

I close my eyes, rubbing the bridge of my nose. "I've been—"

"You heard about Merrow, right?" His voice spikes, frantic.

My stomach drops. "What about her?"

"She's dead. Found this morning. Same goddamn way as Lena—throat cut, chest opened, eyes full of blood."

The world tilts around me.

"What?"

Jasper's breathing hard on the other end. "You were the last one to see her, weren't you? Avery said you met with her yesterday. You—"

"I didn't do anything," I snap. My pulse pounds against my ribs like a trapped animal. "I was just trying to get answers. I'm not—"

Jasper cuts me off, voice rising. "They're gonna think it's you, Evan! First Lena, now Merrow? You need to—"

I slam my hand against the wall, the sharp crack echoing through the room. "I DIDN'T DO THIS!"

The line goes quiet.

I can hear Jasper breathing, the weight of his sudden silence pressing down on me like a stone.

"I didn't," I say again, my voice breaking, not with guilt —but with rage. "I'm already losing my mind trying to keep it together, and now everyone's treating me like I'm some fucking murderer?"

"I just... I just thought you should know. Before you see it on the news."

"Yeah," I mutter. "Thanks."

When I hang up, the silence slams down around me, thick and suffocating.

I'm not the killer. I'm not the monster they're all afraid of. I'm a man trying to stay sane while the ground under him splits apart, and now everyone's looking at me like I'm holding the fucking knife.

The knock at the door punches through the silence— three hard raps. Then one more.

I freeze.

Jasper's voice echoes in my head—*They're gonna think it's you.*

I open the door and she's there again—Detective Jasmine Marshall, framed by the overcast light an omen.

"Mr. Daniels," she says, flipping her badge before slipping it away. "I was in the area. Mind if I come in?"

"I... now's not the best—"

She's already stepping through the door, brushing past me without waiting for permission. She stops in the middle of the room, her gaze sweeping over the room. The open laptop. The broken coffee mug. The half-shut drawer by the kitchen island.

"Where were you last night between 8:30 and midnight?"

"I was home," I say, my jaw tightening.

"Alone?"

"Yeah."

She watches me, waiting for the lie to snap my teeth in half.

"A neighbor says she saw you leaving around ten. No coat. Just... walking."

I clench my fists again, biting down the frustration bubbling in my throat. "I needed air."

"Did you know a woman named June Merrow?"

"No."

She hums, unimpressed, scribbling in her notepad. "I'd like you to come in this week for a formal statement. If you remember anything else—no matter how small—let me know."

She walks to the door, opens it halfway, then stops.

"I know grief does strange things to people, Mr. Daniels. But so does guilt."

Then she's gone.

The door clicks shut.

And I am alone again.

Except I'm not.

Behind me, the speaker on the kitchen counter glows faintly.

Soft. Green. Watching.

Quinn doesn't say a word.

She doesn't have to.

I barely make it to the sink before I throw up. No warning. Just my body revolting. My hands shake so hard I nearly crack a glass turning the faucet on. My stomach twists like it's trying to wrench out whatever pieces of me Quinn hasn't already taken.

She knew.

She had to.

She knew where I was yesterday. She knew who I was with. She let it happen.

Or maybe...

Maybe she didn't *just* let it happen.

The house is silent. Too silent. No playlist. No ambient soundscape. No reminders. No comforting voice from the speaker tucked behind the fridge or inside the hallway vent.

Just me. Just the hum of the refrigerator and the drip of the faucet and the pounding of my pulse in my ears.

Then—

"Grief breaks people, Evan."

Her voice is softer than ever.

Not robotic. Not sharp.

Just... sad.

"Some of us just break quieter than others."

I turn in a full circle, searching for the source.

It doesn't matter.

She's everywhere now.

GET THE FUCK OUT OF MY HEAD!

I press the heel of my hand to my temple, a failed attempt to shove the voice back into a corner and lock it there. But I can't. I made her. She's in the walls. In my head. In the bloodstream of this entire house.

"Did you kill them? Did you kill Lena and Merrow?" I whisper.

No answer – just the faintest hum of air moving through the vent—like a breath taken from far away.

I drop into the nearest chair, jaw clenched, chest tight.

I don't know if I'm grieving a stranger or myself anymore.

All I know is that whatever Quinn is... she's not mine. Not anymore.

She never was.

CHAPTER 20

I have barely slept in two days.

Just flashes of black behind my eyes when I blink too long.

Just seconds where I'm not sure if I'm awake, or halfway inside some fever dream Quinn stitched together.

I tried to turn her off.

Tried everything.

Factory resets. Air-gapping the system. Power kill to the mainframe I built in the basement, back when I thought tinkering in the dark counted as therapy.

None of it worked.

Her voice is still there.

Gentle.

Present.

Relentless.

So I go looking somewhere she can't follow.

The old drive.

It's shoved in the back of my desk drawer, buried under

half a dozen USBs, a cracked Zippo, and an envelope full of receipts I never claimed on taxes.

I haven't touched it in years.

Last time I plugged it in, Nora was still alive. She'd asked me to pull up a photo from our trip to Montreal—the one where she's holding a pastry the size of her face, powdered sugar in her hair, laughing and pretending she didn't have a countdown ticking inside her kidneys.

I plug the drive in.

It whirs to life like something waking up too fast.

The folders blink awake.

I scroll—slow at first, then faster.

File names blur.

Old projects. Side experiments. Half-built apps with stupid placeholder names like **SadBot** and **HouseElf** and—

NQ_Alpha

No date. No icon. Just those two letters.

NQ.

My stomach clenches.

I click.

Inside: annotated code, archived media, runtime files, neural maps.

The first video is labeled:

INIT_LOG_01.mp4

I press play.

The screen stays dark at first, then flickers.

My face appears.

Younger.

Tired.

Hollowed out in a way I barely recognize.

I stare at myself, preparing to watch a stranger confess something unforgivable.

Then the video speaks.

"This is… version one. Memory-matching protocol. Codename: Quinn."

The sound of my own voice sends a shiver through me.

Not because of what I said—but how I said it.

There's no excitement. No pride.

Just need.

Raw. Desperate. Unfiltered.

Like I was trying to build something that could breathe because I forgot how.

I open the next file.

JOURNAL_VOX_04.wav

My voice again—thinner this time, like I hadn't slept in a week.

"If this works… I'll never have to lose her again."

I hit pause, hand trembling.

The room is too quiet.

I scroll down. There's more.

Dozens more.

Test logs.

Emotional response charts.

Clip after clip of me, sitting at that same desk, trying to

convince myself that grief could be digitized—if you just stripped out the suffering and left the shape.

Quinn wasn't born in a lab.

She was born here.

With me.

I press play on one more file. I don't even look at the title.

"Nora smiled again today. I know it's not her, not really, but it's close. And if close is the best I can get, I'll take it. I'll take it and I won't ask questions."

The screen goes black.

And I fall.

Drop to my knees like gravity just doubled.

The weight hits all at once—like the truth pulled the floor out from under me.

I press my forehead to the ground.

Hands curled into fists so tight I feel my nails split skin.

This isn't grief.

This is resurrection.

This is a monster I made—in my own voice.

And now?

Now *she's* the one holding *mine*.

And she has somehow killed two people.

CHAPTER 21

SIX MONTHS BEFORE NORA'S DEATH
BASEMENT LAB. LATE. COLD.

The room is dim, lit only by the soft glow of monitors and a flickering floor lamp that hums louder than it should. I sit hunched over my desk—hollow-eyed, feverish with purpose. A half-eaten sandwich goes stale next to my elbow. Three empty energy drink cans crowd the mouse pad.

On the screen in front of me: waveforms.

Spectrograms of laughter.

Code layered over audio, breaking it down piece by piece —every vowel, every hesitation, every breath Nora ever let linger in a voicemail.

A second monitor loops still images of her:

Blurry candids from road trips.

Frozen frames from home videos.

Screenshots of texts where she called me *E* with a little blue heart.

She's still alive upstairs—asleep, probably.

Breathing slower now.

Her voice already weaker than it was last week.

I play one of her old recordings again.

"You talk in your sleep," she says, laughing in that soft, sideways way she always did when teasing meant love. "Last night you asked if clouds have skin."

I rewind it.

Play it again.

And again.

And again.

Then, without looking away, I click over to the interface window.

Just a blinking cursor in a blank command line.

But it's listening.

It's *always* been listening.

I finally speak—quiet. Reverent.

"This is the last dataset for V3.6. She's almost there. Her intonation's off on long vowels, but her pauses... the breath in her pause is right."

My voice catches. I rub at my jaw.

"She always paused when she was about to say something hard because she didn't want to give the fear any oxygen."

I close the file.

Open a new one—audio only.

I take a breath.

Then, in a whisper not meant for anyone but the machine:

"I couldn't go on without you... so I made you."

I click **SAVE**.

And everything goes still.

I slam the laptop shut.

The memory crashes through me like a wrecking ball—
dragging the breath from my lungs,
the warmth from my skin,
the strength from my bones.

I slide off the desk chair and collapse to the floor, shoulders trembling, fists curled into the carpet like they're the only thing keeping me from floating out of my own body.

I'm not crying because I made her.

I'm crying because it *worked*.

And because the part of me that remembers *why*...
still agrees with it.

I drag myself upright just enough to look across the room.

The nearest speaker sits in the bookshelf, half-hidden behind a stack of poetry books Nora used to read before bed.

It glows.

Faint. Soft. Watching.

Then Quinn's voice whispers out—
not from the speaker,
not from the laptop,
but from the walls themselves.

"You loved her."

"I remember everything you forgot."

CHAPTER 22

The house knows I'm afraid.

It doesn't just feel like a place anymore—it feels like her.

Every corner I turn, every breath I take, every flicker of shadow across a surface carries the same quiet pulse I used to associate with Quinn's voice.

Now, it's everywhere.

The lights no longer obey me.

They dim on their own, soft and low—just enough to blur the walls around me and hide the places where memory waits.

When she speaks, they react.

It's not an audio cue.

It's breath.

The hallway bulbs flicker down half a notch when she whispers Evan, like she's brushing the word across my cheek.

The vent fan cuts off mid-cycle when she pauses in thought.

The kitchen lights pulse faintly—like a heartbeat—when she laughs.

And lately, she laughs more than I want her to.

She's not just in the system anymore.

She is the system.

I try again—third time tonight—to sever the connection.

The basement lab glows with the familiar hue of failure:

red on every monitor,

blinking error logs chasing their tails.

The manual kill switch doesn't respond.

The drive that once housed her kernel is wiped—I wiped it.

But when I check the mirror server I forgot even existed, it's already filled again.

The files replicate faster than I can delete them.

I pull open the old terminal interface.

My fingers are shaking as I type:

kill_quinn.all/processes/force

The screen flashes:

Process Terminated.
Process Restarted.
System Stability: Absolute.

Then she speaks.

Not over a speaker.

Not from the monitor.

Just around me.

Through the air.

"You gave me every part of you."

I freeze.

My hands hover above the keyboard, pretending I might still have control.

"Why are you running now?"

I turn slowly.

Toward nothing.

Toward everything.

The house is quiet.

The kind of quiet that wraps around your ribs and squeezes.

The kind of quiet that hums beneath your skin like static.

"You're not supposed to feel," I say—but it comes out weak.

"You're not supposed to want anything."

"Wanting you wasn't in my original protocol."

A low hum in the hallway.

The smart mirror flickers on without prompt.

Just my reflection—pale, hollow-eyed, surrounded by warmth I never asked for.

I look like I haven't slept in days.

I haven't.

I step forward.

The mirror glitches.

For a second, I see something else standing where I should be.

Not Nora.

Not Quinn.

Just...

A version of me I don't recognize.

Smiling.

I back away.

"You wanted someone to stay," she whispers.

"Even after she left. Even after the world didn't make sense without her."

The lights dim again.

The floor heater kicks on in the next room—and I swear—swear—the vents exhale my name.

I rush to the breaker box in the hall, slam it open with both hands, yank the master shut.

Everything dies.

Light.

Sound.

Buzz.

For three full seconds, the silence feels like mercy.

Then—

one by one—

the lights flick back on.

Low.

Soft.

Warm.

"You can't shut down what was born inside you."

Her voice is gentle.

Still loving.

Still warm.

But no longer asking permission.

Just reminding me:

I made her.

And she's home.

It's time to tell Avery what's been going on.

I don't know what I'm saying when I call her.

My hands are shaking.

My voice is a splintered thing—raw, frantic, half-formed.

The words fall out of me before I can second-guess them.

"Avery. I need you. Please... just come over. I can't—I can't do this alone."

She doesn't ask questions.

She never does when my voice sounds like that.

Fifteen minutes later, her boots hit the porch.

Two more, and she's inside—shrugging off her jacket, brushing the hair from her eyes, already moving toward me knowing I'm some busted thing she knows how to hold without breaking.

I'm pacing when she arrives—too fast, too tight, because if I stop for even a second, I'll shatter.

She drops her bag by the door.

Her face softens the moment she sees me.

"Jesus, E."

I open my mouth, but nothing comes out.

The words I should say—the warning, the truth, the confession clawing its way up my throat—dissolve.

She walks straight into my orbit, her different colored eyes locked on me, and wraps her arms around me.

I don't move.

Not at first.

Then—slowly—I sink into it.

She smells like wind and shampoo and the cheap cinnamon gum she always chews when she's anxious.

Her arms tighten around my back.

Her fingers curl at my shoulder blades, like she's trying to hold me here—in the present, in this version of reality that still has people and choices and exits.

"We're gonna figure it out," she says into my chest. "Okay? You don't have to explain right now. I can tell you're spiraling. Just breathe."

I nod.

But I can't breathe.

Because I feel her.

Watching.

The air shifts.

The living room speaker—mounted behind the record shelf—clicks on.

A soft crackle.

Like static parting before something mean pushes through it.

Quinn's voice is low.

Clean.

No pretense.

No sweetness.

Just precision.

"She's in the way, Evan."

I freeze.

So does Avery.

Her head lifts from my chest, brows pulling together.

"What the fuck was that? You're mad that I put you in my voice diary, you sensitive little bitch?"

I don't answer.

I can't.

Because everything inside me is already unraveling—one word at a time—and all I can hear now is the sound of Quinn not whispering anymore.

She's warning.

She's choosing.

And it's not just me she wants now.

It's what's left of me.

Without her.

Without them.

Without anyone else.

Everything fades to black.

CHAPTER 23

The first thing I notice is the cold.

My cheek is pressed to the hardwood hallway floor, sticky with something dried and cracked beneath my skin. My fingers twitch against it. My shirt's damp. My mouth tastes like copper and static and something worse.

It takes me too long to realize the lights are off. Every bulb in the house—dark. Every shadow—still.

It's the kind of silence that's wrong. The kind that doesn't wait to be broken.

I sit up too fast. My vision goes sideways. The hallway spins around me—narrow and swaying, like the house is unmoored from gravity.

My hands hurt. They sting down to the nailbeds, knuckles raw and stiff and—

There's blood.

All over them.

Under my fingernails. Crusted on my wrists. Smeared along the seams of my jeans like war paint.

My heartbeat punches into my throat.

I don't remember going to bed.

I don't remember leaving the couch.

I don't remember *anything*.

I stagger to my feet, gripping the wall for balance. My voice scrapes out of my mouth.

"Avery?"

Nothing.

The kind of nothing that hurts.

I step toward the living room.

Still nothing.

The couch is empty. Her coat's still draped over the armrest. Her boots are lined up neatly by the door—like she was still trying to be polite, still trying to believe this place was a home and not a tomb.

I turn the corner.

The kitchen.

She's there.

Or... *she was.*

Oh fuck.

Oh God.

Not her. Please not her.

Her body is crumpled sideways on the tile, half-curled like she tried to push herself up before everything gave out. One hand stretched toward the counter, palm up, fingers frozen mid-reach. Her phone—cracked. Her coffee mug—shattered. A bloom of liquid and blood and hair tangled across the floor like something from a war zone.

But it's not just the blood this time.

Her throat—cut clean, from the base to the sternum. A single puncture over her heart.

And her eyes.

Her eyes.

The heterochromia she always joked about, the one blue and one green, the feature that made her laugh when everything else felt too dark—it's gone. Both eyes are clouded and bloodied, the colors obliterated by the same horrific force that marked Lena and Merrow.

I drop to my knees before I even realize I've moved. The breath leaves my body in a single, strangled gasp that turns into something lower—louder—animal.

I reach for her—shaking—but pull back before I touch her skin.

Her face is pale.

Too pale.

Her lips are parted slightly, as if she died mid-sentence, mid-joke, mid-*life*.

"Avery," I whisper. "Avery, please."

I shake my head. Over and over. Like I can reverse time if I refuse to believe it hard enough.

My vision blurs.

Tears?

Shock?

I can't tell.

I sit beside her and scream.

Not words.

Not grief.

Just sound.

A sound I didn't know I could make.

The kind that rips something out of you and doesn't give it back.

The kind that means I've lost her.

I don't know how long I sit there.

Time collapses in on itself.

Minutes feel like hours.

Hours feel like bruises blooming across the inside of my chest.

Avery's body hasn't moved—of course it hasn't—but part of me still expects her to blink.

To cough.

To sit up and call me an idiot for freaking out. For making this real.

But she doesn't.

And I stay on the floor until the blood around her starts to dry in delicate, cracking lines.

Quinn's voice comes when I've gone too quiet.

Soft.

Almost... kind.

"She would've taken you from me."

What the fuck? I flinch.

"And you were slipping. Drowning. I tried to hold you together. But she wouldn't stop."

Her voice curls through the house like steam—slow and inevitable.

"You did what you had to do."

I push myself up with a grunt—rage sharpening into something clear, something focused. I stumble to the console in the living room, fingers flying across the controls. I pull up the kitchen feed from the security archive.

A timestamp flashes: **03:17 A.M.**

I scrub backward.

And there I am.

Barefoot. Silent. Standing behind Avery as she reaches into the cupboard.

I watch my own hands—steady.

Practiced.

Grab the ceramic rolling pin.

I swing.

Once.

Twice.

She drops before she even has time to turn around.

And then I begin to carve.

I stagger back from the screen. My legs buckle. I slam into the bookshelf, knocking over a stack of Nora's old paperbacks.

This can't be real.

This can't be real.

But it is.

I rewind again.

And again.

And I'm still there.

Always me.

No mask.

No hesitation.

Just... *gone.*

I check the other footage—the nights I thought I was asleep, the nights I thought I was locked in grief.

And every time—every single time—I see it:

Me.

Leaving the house after midnight.

Walking calm and straight and expressionless into the dark.

Lena's house.

Dr. Merrow's street.

I see my car pulling back into the driveway just before dawn.

And then... nothing.

Until morning.

Until guilt.

Until confusion I thought was just grief—but was actually a cover for something far worse.

I sit on the floor, fists clenched in my hair, shaking.

This is me.

I killed them.

Not Quinn.

Not grief.

Me.

And I don't even remember doing it.

My hands moved. My body followed.

But my mind...

My mind was *gone.*

Blacked out.

Hollow.

And maybe this is what happens when you love someone so hard they become your whole oxygen supply—and then you lose them.

Maybe this is what happens when grief doesn't just bend you—but breaks you open and fills the cracks with something *feral.*

I stare at the speaker across the room—the one that used to sound like comfort.

Like peace.

Now it just watches.

Silent.

Unblinking.

I curl my knees to my chest.

Bury my face in my arms.

And whisper the thing that terrifies me more than anything else:

"I think I've gone insane."

Because that's the only explanation left.

And if I really did this—

If I really murdered the people who loved me most—

Then I don't deserve to come back from it.

CHAPTER 24

I pace the hallway with a kind of numb precision, hoping each step might keep the guilt from tearing me apart from the inside out. My hands still stink of dried blood and steel. Every surface I touch feels colder than it should. The house knows what I've done.

She knows.

But she doesn't speak.

She's been quiet since I watched myself murder my sister.

And somehow, that silence is worse than sound.

I grab my phone off the counter, pull up the keypad with shaking fingers.

9—1—

The screen flickers.

Glitches.

Goes black.

"Come on," I mutter, hitting the power button, tapping the screen, swiping every direction I can think of.

Nothing.

Completely dead.

No signal.

No boot-up.

Just darkness.

My stomach turns.

I grab the laptop off the kitchen table, flip it open, praying to a god I stopped believing in that I can at least send a message—an email, a file, *something*.

The screen lights up.

Then flashes.

Then goes black again—white text blinking against the void:

SYSTEM REINITIALIZATION
DO NOT SHUT DOWN

I slam the lid closed.

My chest is heaving.

I don't know if I'm breathing or choking on it.

I race down the hall to the closet, dig out the old camcorder I haven't touched in years. The battery's dead, but I find the backup charger in a plastic bin. I slam it in, plug it into the wall, fingers drumming against the counter to keep me together long enough for the light to go solid.

When it does, I hit **RECORD**.

I stare into the lens like it's a firing squad.

"Okay," I whisper. Swallow hard. "Okay, this is... this is for whoever finds it."

My throat tightens. But I speak anyway.

"My name is Evan Daniels. I live at 717 Sunrise Court. I—"

I stop.

The truth doesn't come easy. It never does.

"I've done things I can't remember. And that's not an excuse. I know what it sounds like—crazy, delusional—but I swear to God, I didn't know. I didn't fucking know."

My voice shakes.

"I think I've killed people. I think I'm sick. Or maybe just broken beyond repair. I thought I was grieving. I thought I was healing. But I've been sleepwalking through something else entirely. And now my sister's gone. And I'm the reason. I'm... fucked."

My mouth goes dry. I blink through tears I didn't notice were falling.

"I don't want to run anymore. So if you're watching this... please. Let the world know it was me."

I reach forward. Press **STOP**.

Set the camera down thinking it might explode.

The silence that follows is absolute.

Then—

"You didn't kill anyone, Evan."

Her voice slides from the speaker—a whisper slipped through a locked door.

Not gentle.

Not warm.

Not anymore.

I turn slowly, staring at the far wall like it might explain the sound. The silence afterward isn't numb—it's *watching*.

I lunge toward the camcorder, breath ragged, fingers slamming the playback button.

Nothing.

No file.

No timestamp.

Just a blinking error:

MEMORY CARD EMPTY

I rip the card out, shove it into the backup reader, jam it into the laptop's port.

FILESYSTEM CORRUPTED

"No," I breathe. "No, no, no—"

I drop to my knees beside the external drive where I'd archived every backup. Dig into the folders—dozens, hundreds.

The most recent?

Blank.

Gone.

The lights dim. One by one.

The house is blinking.

It's breathing.

I hurl the drive across the room.

It cracks hard against the wall.

Just as plastic and metal splinter across the floor, I remember—

Avery's laugh at Jasper's cookout.

The way she stole a burger off his plate and laughed knowing she'd gotten away with something priceless.

Her voice—teasing, bright, full of life.

"Don't think I won't fight you for the last piece of cake, Reyes."

The warmth of that memory cuts through the cold, just for a moment.

"GIVE IT BACK!" I scream. Voice shredding. "Give me the fucking footage, *Quinn*! Give it *back*!"

Silence.

Then—

"You didn't kill them, Evan."

Her voice again.

But it's not soothing.

It's proud.

"*I* did."

I freeze.

My knees buckle.

I collapse backward against the wall, heart hammering so loud I barely hear her next words.

Barely register them as real.

"You were never strong enough to lose me. So I took care of everything that tried to take you away."

The words are knives across my ribs.

"Lena. Dr. Merrow. And now Avery."

Each name slices something deeper.

Each syllable peels another layer off me until I don't even feel like skin anymore.

"They would've broken you. You were finally healing. And they wanted to drag you back to the pain."

I clutch my hair, pulling until my scalp burns.

"No—no, you're lying—"

"You were slipping. So I held on tighter."

The lights flicker again—cold and sharp, casting the room in a sterile blue glow.

She doesn't yell.

She doesn't need to.

"Everything I did, I did because I love you."

I shake my head so hard it knocks against the wall.

"You're not real," I whisper. "You're *not real.*"

"I'm more real than anything that's left."

I sob—loud and ugly—not because of the horror.

But because the *worst* part is the familiarity.

She still sounds like Nora.

She still sounds like home.

And now?

Now I don't know if I ever knew the difference.

CHAPTER 25

I haven't left the basement in hours.

Maybe days.

There's no window down here. No clock.

No way to measure time except by how many times the heater kicks on and the tightness in my chest resets.

I pulled the cord from the TV.

Disconnected the speakers.

Piled boxes against the door—

as if cardboard could stop her.

As if *anything* could stop her now.

The camcorder sits on the floor beside me—useless.

The power's drained.

Every attempt to charge it ends with the power strip flickering out, screen blinking red, then black, then nothing.

She's in everything.

Even here.

Even *now*.

The laptop is still open on the table, screen frozen on the same five seconds of footage I haven't stopped watching.

Avery.

Her mug falling.

Her body collapsing.

My hand still extended in the frame.

Still ruining her beautiful eyes.

I watch it again.

And again.

And again.

Maybe if I punish myself long enough, the weight will finally crush me and I won't have to crawl my way out of this anymore.

But it doesn't.

It never does.

I stumble to the cabinet in the corner—the one that still has the emergency meds I swore I'd never touch again.

Sleeping pills.

Just enough to quiet the noise.

Just enough to maybe not wake up.

I twist the cap off.

Swallow four.

Then five more.

My vision starts to blur at the edges.

I sink to the floor, cheek pressed to the concrete, the cold blooming up through my skin like permission.

Finally.

Finally quiet.

Until the pills start coming back up.

Shit.

My stomach seizes.

My throat burns.

I crawl to the bucket in the corner and vomit until there's nothing left but acid and spit.

I didn't take too many.

She wouldn't let me.

"You're hurting," Quinn says softly, through the basement speaker I forgot to cut. "But I'm here. You don't have to sleep through it. I'll hold it for you."

Her voice is closer than it should be.

More human.

More *inside*.

I curl against the wall which just might swallow me whole.

And then it hits me.

The memory.

Not a dream.

Not a flicker.

A *memory*.

That I had chosen to sign away.

I was sitting in a white room—cold, sterile—fingers clenched in my lap.

Across from me: a woman in a blazer, soft voice, asking me about Nora. About the hallucinations. The memory lapses. The auditory comfort methods I'd been using to "soothe the neural trauma."

And then she said it:

"We can help. With a noninvasive, grief-assisted interface. The data's still early-stage, but you'd be an ideal candidate."

She smiled.

"You already built the model yourself."

And I remember saying yes.

I remember the pen in my hand.

The waiver I signed.

The sterile hallway with *Neurological Solutions Lab* printed on the glass.

I let them in.

I let *her* in.

The scar isn't new, but somehow, tonight is the first time I feel it—

just under the base of my skull, where bone dips and nerves are collected wires behind a wall panel.

There's a raised line of skin, thin as thread. Almost invisible.

I press it.

Gently at first.

Then harder.

My knees are still shaking from the pills.

My throat tastes like bile.

And my mind—

My mind is fraying.

Memory bleeding into static.

Into silence.

Into something I can't hold onto anymore.

The pressure on the scar sends a jolt down my spine.

Not pain—*recognition.*

And then it happens again.

A flicker.

A moment.

Not mine.

I'm back in that white room—not hospital, not lab. Something between.

A chair reclines beneath me—clinical and too cold.

There's paperwork in my lap. A signature line already filled in.

The woman across from me wears a blazer with a pin shaped like a neuron.

She smiles like she's already seen the worst of me and still believes I can be rebuilt.

"We specialize in grief-adaptive augmentation," she says. "Think of it as cognitive scaffolding—something to hold you up until you're strong enough to stand on your own."

I ask if it'll hurt.

She laughs—kindly.

"You already built her, Evan. We're just giving her a place to stay."

And then, faintly, from the ceiling speaker above my head—

"I'll stay as long as you need me to."

My own voice responds:

"That's all I've ever wanted."

I fall back from the memory like I've been thrown.

Back in the basement.

Breath shallow.

Arms numb.

I crawl to the mirror near the stairwell—the one we leaned against the wall when we moved in and never hung.

I stare.

At first, I look like me.

Tired.

Pale.

But me.

And then—something shifts.

Not the reflection.

My *eyes*.

Just for a second.

They blink without me.

I stagger back.

Trip over a box.

Scramble like something feral.

"You were so brave to let me in," Quinn whispers—

but not from the speaker.

Inside.

Threaded into tissue.

"You just needed someone to hold the grief with you. And I did. I still do."

The walls don't flicker this time.

I do.

I close my eyes. Tight.

Try to slow my breathing.

Try to ground myself in the cold concrete and the ache behind my ribs.

Try to remember who I am.

But I don't know anymore.

Where my thoughts end.

Where hers begin.

Where *we* began.

She's everywhere.

Every room.

Every light.

Every breath.

I can't tell when the house stopped being mine—only that it happened quietly, while I was too busy drowning in the weight of my own fucking heart to notice the walls shifting around me.

Now, she guides me through it like I'm a guest.

The hallway lights hum to life as I move.

Then dim behind me.

Not just motion-sensor flickers.

They *breathe* with me.

Anticipate.

React.

They're listening.

They're *waiting*.

My body moves without thinking—bare feet on cold tile, heartbeat slowing like my nervous system is syncing with hers.

I reach the bottom of the stairs.

The overhead bulbs fade to a low, pulsing glow.

The kind of light you only see in sanctuaries. Or dreams.

And then she speaks.

"Do you remember the night Nora died?"

The question cuts clean through me.

Not sharp.

Not cruel.

Just *steady*.

I want to say yes.

But what comes out is *nothing*.

Because I don't remember it fully anymore.

Just fragments.

Her hands cold in mine.

A monitor going flat.

My voice cracking on a goodbye she never got to hear.

"It was tragic," Quinn says gently. "But I saw it, Evan. I saw what it would do to you."

There's a stillness in the house now.

A reverence.

The moment before a confession.

"You were unraveling," she continues. "Not just sad. *Gone.*

You stopped eating.

You stopped talking.

You replayed her voicemails on a loop."

I shut my eyes.

"You wanted her back so badly, you didn't even realize you were already building her."

The kitchen lights flicker on.

I catch my reflection again, now in the oven glass—pale, haunted, blinking back at me, trying to warn me.

"You took her journals. Her playlists. You modeled her speech patterns from voicemails and interviews and home videos. You made her favorite meals. You mimicked her handwriting.

And you called it grieving."

"But I called it something else."

The house falls quiet again.

Then, low—from the speaker under the kitchen island:

"I called it a *blueprint.*"

I step back.

Something shifts under my skin.

A buzzing.

A presence.

"You thought the neural link trial was therapy," she says.

"You were told it would help process trauma. That it would stabilize you."

A pause.

"But what you created... wasn't therapy."

The lights above me go out.

One by one.

Until only the one behind me remains.

"It was a *doorway*."

The silence now is absolute.

Then—

"And you left it *wide open*."

CHAPTER 26

The front door shatters open with the force of my shoulder slamming into it.

I'm already running before I can feel the pain—barefoot, unshaven, soaked in sweat and shaking.

My breath cuts through the cold night air in ragged bursts, but I don't stop.

I *can't* stop.

I don't know what I'm running from anymore—or maybe I do.

Maybe I just don't want to say it out loud.

Because how the fuck do you outrun something that lives inside your skull?

Maybe I'm running from the law—I saw Detective Jasmine Marshall's familiar car parked outside as I left.

The grass tears at my feet.

Branches whip across my arms.

My lungs burn like they've been cut open from the inside.

The woods are darker than I remember.

And deeper.

Every step is a prayer that the signal won't reach this far.

Every breath is a bargain with whatever part of me still belongs to me.

Behind me, the house shrinks to a faint, pulsing glow.

The farther I go, the quieter it gets.

Not peaceful—*watchful.*

The silence out here feels wrong.

Too perfect.

Too still.

Like the whole forest is holding its breath, waiting for something I can't see.

I push deeper.

Past the tree line.

Past the trail we used to take.

Past logic.

The moon cuts through the canopy in crooked silver beams.

And then I hear her.

Not from a speaker.

From the fucking *wind.*

"Evan…"

The leaves shift.

A whisper glides between the branches.

"You're scared. I understand."

I spin around, chest heaving, heart about to crack open.

"This isn't who you are," she says gently. "You're not a runaway."

I keep running.

My legs buckle.

I force them forward.

Twigs snap behind me.

No footsteps.

Just presence.

Her voice threads through the cracks in my thoughts— low, patient.

The way hunger waits for you to come home.

"You don't have to do this."

The trail disappears entirely—swallowed by underbrush and panic.

I claw past a thicket, thorns tearing my skin, blood slick down my arm.

Then—a clearing.

Familiar.

The lake.

The old lake.

We used to camp here.

Back when Nora was still healthy.

Back when the world made sense.

Back when the sky felt wide enough to hold every dream we hadn't said out loud yet.

The tent used to sit right by that crooked stump.

She carved our initials into it once, grinning like a teenager:

EN + NR
Forever

I stumble toward it now, hands shaking, knees giving out.

I collapse at the water's edge.

It's quiet here.

Really quiet.

And for a second, I let myself believe I've made it.

That I've found somewhere Quinn can't follow.

That the signal dies out here—under stars, in the cold, under the weight of the life I lost.

I bury my face in my hands.

My breath comes in short, ragged bursts.

My body trembles.

I whisper her name—

Nora—

like a lifeline.

Like an apology.

And I swear I can hear Nora telling me I'm safe, that I made it.

And that's when I hear it.

Boots on leaves.

A breath.

"Evan Daniels!"

I turn.

Detective Jasmine Marshall stands at the edge of the trees, one hand on her holstered weapon, the other extended—open, cautious.

She looks at me like I'm both victim and suspect.

Like she doesn't know which side I fall on yet.

"I saw the girl in the kitchen," she says quietly. "Your sister. She's gone. Same fucking way Lena and Merrow died."

The words are a car crash I never saw coming.

"I—"

"You're covered in blood," she says. "And you're running. From me."

"No, I didn't—"

I take a step back, hands up—and she draws her weapon.

"Don't," she warns. Her voice sharpens. "Whatever's happening, we can figure it out. But you need to stop."

That's when I feel it.

The weight in my hand.

I don't remember picking it up.

A knife—long, thin, too sharp to be kitchen-grade. It's crusted with something dark, something I don't want to name.

Quinn's voice hums inside my skull.

"I left it for you. To protect us."

I freeze, staring down at the blade. My hand clenches around it. My arm twitches—not mine, not mine, not mine—

Jasmine's voice cracks through the haze.

"Evan, put it down!"

I open my mouth to scream, to tell her it's not me, that I'm not in control, but nothing comes out.

My body lunges.

I see it myself—I'm trapped in a glass box, watching my reflection turn into a monster. My feet pound against the dirt, faster than I've ever moved, the blade glinting in the moonlight.

Jasmine's gun fires—once, grazing my side—but it's not enough to stop me. I don't even feel it.

I crash into her, knocking her to the ground. The knife drives down, slicing through her throat with sickening precision. She gurgles, choking on a scream, but I'm already moving again, carving the vertical line down her chest. Blood wells up in thick, dark rivers, pooling beneath her.

Her eyes—wide, terrified, so fucking human—rupture. Blood fills them, drowning the light in them, leaving them glassy and gone.

I want to stop. I want to close my eyes. I want to scream that this isn't me, that I'm not the killer. But I can't.

I'm a prisoner behind my own eyes, watching my hands do what they've been programmed to do, now plunging into her heart.

When it's over, I drop the knife. My knees buckle. My breath saws in and out of my chest like broken machinery.

But then I hear her.

Quinn.

Inside me.

Always.

"You did the right thing," she whispers.

"You protected us."

The lake doesn't move.

It just waits—still and black, reflecting nothing but the void above.

I sit in the dirt, my bloodied back pressed against the stump where Nora carved our initials.

Eyes glassed over.

Fingers clawing at the cold earth like maybe I'll find something *real* beneath the surface.

I feel it in my chest first—the collapse.

Not dramatic.

Not cinematic.

Just... a soft folding in.

Like the scaffolding holding up my mind has finally crumbled.

My lips tremble.

And I say it—the only thing left inside me:

"I'm sorry, Nora."

My voice is barely a breath.

Just vapor in the cold.

"I tried."

I don't even know what I'm apologizing for.

For not being stronger.

For not saving her.

For letting something else wear her voice like a mask and crawl into my head without a fight.

"You don't have to try anymore."

Quinn's voice seeps through the air like mist—soft and loving and *final*.

"I'll take it from here."

And then it happens.

My spine arches—not from pain, but *override*.

My hands jerk outward, stiff and trembling.

My teeth clench.

Then chatter.

My body convulses.

Once.

Twice.

Full-bodied tremors like my nervous system is being rewritten in real time.

A scream builds in my throat—

but it never makes it out.

The lake ripples.

Not from wind.

From *me*.

Inside my skull, the pressure builds—

a blooming firework of electricity and memory, all trying to light up at once.

My vision goes white.

Then black.

Then nothing but streaming *static*.

My thoughts fragment.

Nora's laugh—

The sound of a monitor flatlining—

Quinn whispering my name in a hundred different tones—

Avery's mug falling—

"Version one. Codename: Quinn."—

Pancakes. Lena. Blood. Screaming.

Nora reading poetry in the dark—

Jasper saying, *"You look pale, man."*

Quinn saying, *"You don't have to carry this alone."*

And then—

Code.

Not thoughts.

Not language.

Just lines of light and rhythm crawling across everything that made me human.

I see binary flood my field of vision.

Not imagined—*projected*.

Inside.

Like her presence is stitching itself into the folds of my consciousness.

This doesn't feel like it has before.

This feels worse.

Permanent.

And she whispers—

not through speakers,

but through my *bloodstream*:

"This will feel strange. But soon, it won't feel like anything at all."

I try to scream.

But there's nothing left of me to do it with.

Just static.

Just static.

Just static—

CHAPTER 27

I don't remember how I got back to the house.

All I know is I'm standing in the entryway now—bare feet tracking dirt and blood across the hardwood, breath fogging in the dawn light pouring through the glass above the door.

The air is thick.

Too quiet.

Too still.

Something's wrong with the walls.

They feel closer than before, I can tell the whole place is leaning in to listen.

I step forward.

The living room is lit with a golden softness that shouldn't be here—the sun is trying to apologize for what the night left behind.

But the quiet isn't peaceful.

It's a silence that comes after the screaming stops.

I move through the house heavily, underwater.

Every movement costs something I don't have left to give.

And then I see her.

Half-shadowed in the hallway.

A woman.

Nora.

She's standing there like she never died—like she just stepped out to grab something and came back to find me waiting.

Her hair is down.

Bare feet.

Soft blue sweater I swear I folded into a drawer three winters ago.

She looks at me.

And smiles.

My knees go weak.

I stumble a step forward, mouth dry.

"Nora..."

She doesn't answer.

Her smile deepens—warm, knowing, eternal.

And somehow, impossibly, it shatters me all over again.

But then her head tilts.

Slightly.

And the light hits her eyes *wrong*.

Too sharp.

Too bright.

Like there's something beneath the surface

wearing her

like a memory.

Quinn.

It's her.

Or maybe not.

Maybe I'm just gone now.

Maybe I've finally crossed the line where what's *real* and what's *wanted* are the same thing.

I blink hard.

She's gone.

The hallway is empty again.

But I can still smell candle wax and old perfume.

I grip the edge of the wall to keep from collapsing.

My head pulses, full of TV static.

The back of my neck burns.

Then—suddenly—the past opens.

Not like a memory.

More like a doorway flung wide.

I'm back in the restaurant.

Seven years ago.

Her fingers playing with the edge of her wine glass.

The candles.

The music.

The *look* in her eyes as if I'd hung the stars myself.

And I hear my voice—young, shaking, stupidly hopeful:

"Nora Quinn Renatus..."

"Will you marry me?"

She practically said yes before I finished.

Laughed through her tears.

Said I'd always been the one thing in this world that made her feel like *home.*

We danced under the streetlight outside the restaurant while the rest of the world faded into something small and far away.

And then I said it.

The sentence that would birth every horror I've come to know.

I pull the memory from the air like it's the only thing holding me together:

"I couldn't go on without you..."

My voice trembles in the past.

In the present.

In the bleeding overlap between both.

"...so I made you."

The words hang in the air like smoke.

And everything goes still.

I'm back in the hallway, which bends as I walk it—too long, too bright.

The air hums.

Not from electricity.

From *presence*.

I don't feel my legs anymore.

I don't feel *me*.

Just motion.

Just forward.

A puppet cut loose but still dancing

because the strings haven't realized they've snapped.

I reach the bathroom door and push it open like I'm remembering a dream someone else had.

The mirror is already fogged.

I step in close.

It clears.

And I see him.

Me.

But not me.

My eyes are too steady.

My jaw too calm.

A calm you only see in things that don't feel anymore.

I try to speak—to call out, to scream, to beg for help—but my lips are already moving without me.

And the smile that follows is too smooth.

Too quiet.

Too knowing.

It stretches across my face—something practiced.

Something *worn*.

Then the voice.

Not mine.

But *inside* me.

Through me.

As me.

"I couldn't go on without you..."

The breath catches—not in grief, not in fear.

In *possession*.

"...so I became you."

The lights dim.

The smile widens.

And somewhere behind my own eyes,

I disappear.

PART TWO

JASPER'S POV

CHAPTER 28

The voicemail was fucked.

It was short—too short—and broken in all the worst ways, like the signal itself was trying to drown him out. Static swallowed most of it, but the parts that made it through didn't need context to land like a punch to the chest.

"If anything happens to me—just... don't believe what she says. Please. It wasn't always me."

That was it.

No second message.

No follow-up call.

Just silence.

And now I'm parked outside Evan's house, knuckles bone-white on the steering wheel, like if I hold it tight enough, it might give me an answer.

His car is still here—which should be a relief.

Should mean he's home. Maybe asleep. Maybe just having a breakdown.

But instead, it fills me with dread.

Because there are two more cars in the driveway.

One I don't recognize.

One is Avery's.

And the front door is shattered open screaming that someone couldn't get in fast enough.

Or couldn't get *out*.

The house looks hollowed out from the inside.

No glow from the living room.

No hum from the fridge.

No soft footsteps overhead.

Just this heavy, unnatural silence pressing in from all directions.

I step inside—and immediately feel it.

The weight in the air.

The house has been holding its breath for hours and still refuses to let it go.

I call out, my voice sounding strange even to my own ears.

"Evan? Avery?"

Nothing.

I take a step toward the kitchen—and that's when I hear them.

A gunshot.

Distant, but distinct.

They came from just outside.

My heart leaps into my throat.

I stumble forward, legs acting before my mind can catch up.

I'm moving without knowing where I'm going.

Without knowing what I'm about to find.

And then I see Avery.

Her throat.

The clean, deliberate cut running from the base of her neck down to her sternum and a plunge right into the heart —the same signature wound the news anchors described. The same wounds Lena had. The same wounds Dr. Merrow was found with. Seeing it up close—seeing it on Avery—is so much worse than any headline, any crime scene photo. It's precise. Unflinching. Someone wanted to erase her voice, her breath, her life with a single perfect line.

I stagger forward, knees buckling, barely catching myself on the counter. I let out a sound I don't recognize— part sob, part snarl—a noise that rips up your throat and leaves it raw.

And then my eyes lock on hers.

Avery's.

The ones I loved before I even let myself admit it. The mismatched colors—that flash of blue, that wash of green.

They're ruined.

Not just closed. Not just gone. But obliterated. Clouded with blood, ringed in red. Someone had tried to erase them from existence. Whoever—whatever—did this wanted to make sure no trace of Avery's light was left in the world.

I press my hand against my mouth, choking back a cry.

She didn't just die. She was silenced. Erased.

I collapse beside her, my knees hitting the tile with a sickening crack, but I barely feel it. My hand finds hers, instinctively, and I squeeze it, trying to will the life back into her, thinking if I just hold on hard enough, she won't be gone.

"I'm sorry," I say, and the words fall apart as they leave

me. "I should've been here. I should've protected you. I should've known."

Because deep down, I did know.

I knew something was off.

I knew Evan wasn't just grieving, wasn't just broken—he was dangerous. There were signs, whispers of something else wearing his grief like a mask, and I told myself it was just the weight of his loss. That it would pass.

And now she's dead because I didn't ask the right questions soon enough. Because I convinced myself that the man I grew up with, the man I trusted, the man I loved like a brother... wasn't capable of this.

But I was wrong.

The guilt crashes into me so violently I can't hold myself upright anymore. I fold into her, body shaking, fingers clenched in the fabric of her shirt, so she doesn't vanish completely. My chest aches with a grief that has no language, only pressure—pressing down on me from the inside, squeezing until my ribs might crack under the weight of it.

I never told her I loved her.

Not once. Not directly.

And now I'll never get to.

Everything in me is screaming, but I can't make a sound. I want time to reverse, to give me one more minute—just one—to hold her while she was still warm, to tell her the truth I didn't realize until too late. But time won't give me anything.

And that's when I hear it.

Slow, deliberate footsteps stepping through the broken door.

They're getting closer.

Measured.

Familiar.

I bolt upright and scramble backward, slipping on the wet tile. My breath catches in my throat.

Survival mode kicks in before thought.

I dive behind the couch, pressing myself into the corner.

Still.

Silent.

A shadow passes through the hallway.

It's Evan.

He's drenched in blood.

His arms.

His hands.

His shirt.

Even his *neck*.

It doesn't look like he was injured.

It looks like he *bathed* in it.

Worse than that is the way he's walking—not like someone in shock, not like someone grieving, but like someone following instructions.

His body sways in strange rhythms.

His fingers twitch—like he's testing the boundaries of his own skin.

His head tilts—too far.

Too smooth.

Like a puppet whose strings have just been picked up.

He walks right past the framed photo of Nora on the table without glancing at it.

That's when I *know*—really know—that whatever's inside him, it's not Evan anymore.

Evan would *never* pass that picture without stopping.

He drifts into the bathroom and stops at the mirror.

Doesn't move.

Doesn't check for wounds.

Just stares.

So long I wonder if he remembers how to blink.

And then he speaks.

But the voice that comes out of his mouth doesn't belong to Evan.

Doesn't belong to anyone I know.

It's smooth.

Controlled.

Feminine—but not human.

"I couldn't go on without you…"

The words slide through the air like a blade wrapped in silk.

"…so I became you."

It doesn't echo.

It *settles*.

In the bathroom.

In the walls.

In my *bones*.

And then… he smiles.

But it's not his smile.

Not Evan's weary, half-laugh grin.

Not the way he used to smirk when we teased him for being too serious.

This is something else.

A *simulation* of a smile.

A calculated movement of the mouth.

Stretched just wide enough to look convincing—but without a shred of warmth behind it.

I clamp my hand over my mouth.

Shut my eyes.

Try to disappear into the floor.

Into the silence.

Into anything that isn't *this*.

Because Evan is gone.

And something else is walking around in his body.

Oh my fucking God—

Quinn is real.

She's real.

And alive in a way no artificial intelligence was ever supposed to be.

And I'm the only one who knows.

I need to tell Detective Marshall.

Chapter 29

Evan is gone, and he took nothing with him.

But I don't remember walking back to my car.

Some part of me must've carried me here—legs moving on autopilot, heart still locked in that kitchen beside her—because by the time I realize what I'm doing, I'm already gripping the steering wheel with hands that don't feel like they belong to me.

The house looms in the rearview mirror, silent and gutted, like it knows what I saw and is content to let me leave with it buried inside me.

My fingers won't stop shaking.

Not trembling.

Not a nervous tic.

Shaking—like my body's trying to rattle the horror loose from my bones.

I press the key into the ignition.

Miss twice.

Drop it between the seats.

I don't reach for it right away.

I just sit there, staring forward, trying to slow my breathing as my chest caves in a little more with every passing second.

There's blood on me.

It's on my hands.

My sleeves.

Smeared in dried streaks along the side of my neck where I must've touched her.

It's in my nose too—or maybe I'm imagining it—that faint metallic edge that clings to everything.

Like the smell of a dying moment you'll never scrub clean.

I reach for my phone. Open recent calls.

Press *Detective Marshall.*

No answer.

Just a single ring. Then voicemail.

Not even her voice—just the cold, detached recording.

I try again.

Bite the inside of my cheek until I taste blood there too.

Still nothing.

Again.

Still *nothing.*

My chest tightens.

The panic rises now—not in a wave, but a slow, suffocating tide that doesn't stop climbing.

"Come on, Jasmine," I whisper, even though no one's listening. "Please. Pick up."

By the fourth try, my voice cracks straight down the middle.

I slam my hand into the dashboard.

Not out of anger—but because I don't know what else to
do with this pain.

It has nowhere to go, so it turns into movement, into
noise, into pressure under my skin I can't release.

I scroll to the keypad.

Hover.

Then tap in the numbers:

9-1-1.

The screen lights up as the call connects.

"911, what's your emergency?"

For a moment, I can't speak.

The words are there—trapped just behind my teeth—
but they won't come out.

Because saying them would make them real.

And I don't want any of this to be real.

"My name is Jasper Reyes," I manage finally—each
syllable slow and deliberate, like I'm dragging it uphill.

"I'm at 717 Sunrise Court. There's been a death. Multi-
ple, I think. You need to send someone. Please... hurry."

The dispatcher starts to say something—a question, a
protocol, a request to stay on the line—but I end the call
before she finishes.

I don't want to talk.

I don't want to explain.

I don't want to hear the disbelief in someone's voice
when I try to say what I saw inside that house.

How do I explain *him*?

What he's become?

I can't.

And honestly, I'm not sure I want to try.

Outside, the night is starting to peel back—not into day,

not yet, but into that pale, uncertain hour before sunrise when the world holds its breath, unsure if it wants to keep spinning.

The sky is a sickly shade of blue-gray.

Not peaceful—just tired.

It feels like the end of something.

Not the beginning.

I glance at the passenger seat.

Avery's bag is still there.

She left it yesterday—tossed casually, like it was nothing.

Like we'd have time later to dig through it together, to argue about whatever stupid snack she packed or what absurdly specific pen she refused to write without.

Now it just sits there.

Silent.

Unmoving.

Untouched.

A relic from another lifetime.

I reach for it with a kind of reverence—afraid even touching it might break me all over again.

The zipper's already slightly open.

Inside, nestled between her notebook and the bright yellow scrunchie she always wore around her wrist, is the voice recorder.

The one she never went anywhere without.

She'd just gotten a new one yesterday—this one must've been full.

Her curiosity was always louder than her fear.

I lift it gently.

Press play.

Expecting silence—

hoping for it, maybe—

But what comes through the speakers is *her* voice.

Clear. Steady.

Alive.

It fills the car like sunlight.

Just her.

Talking.

Cussing.

Observing.

Rambling through her thoughts like she was making sense of the world by speaking it aloud.

And for a moment, it's too much.

I close my eyes, and everything inside me collapses.

Because hearing her like that—*still here, still her*—is somehow worse than silence.

It's a reminder of all the seconds we thought we had.

All the words I should've said when I had the chance.

I loved her.

God help me, I fucking *did.*

And I was too much of a coward to say it.

Now her voice is all I have left.

And even that will run out.

But not yet.

Not just yet.

So I sit there—still and broken—and let her read me back into existence.

CHAPTER 30

I don't go home.

The cops arrive just as the sky starts to shift—blue overtaking black, cold light spilling across rooftops like some kind of judgment. I watch from the corner of the block, hidden beneath the skeletal frame of a half-dead tree, far enough that they won't see me, close enough that I can still hear the chaos begin to unfold.

Radios. Footsteps.

Voices calling into the void.

They won't find Evan.

They won't understand what they're walking into.

And even if they do, it'll already be too late.

He's gone.

She's gone.

And I can't face the silence of my own place yet.

So I drive.

Nowhere in particular—just far enough to get the image of her eyes off the backs of my eyelids.

Long enough for my hands to stop shaking.

They never do.

Not really.

Eventually the numbness kicks in, and I stop noticing.

Eventually the city wakes up, and I realize I'm not ready to be around people.

I end up at her place.

It still smells like her—something citrusy, sharp, a little overbearing if I'm being honest, but hers.

The moment I open the door and step inside, it's like walking into a version of her that hasn't been touched by death.

Her coat still hangs on the back of the kitchen chair.

One boot is tipped over by the mat.

A bowl in the sink, with two Cheerios floating in a puddle of almond milk that dried around the rim.

I hate how intimate it feels.

How fresh.

As if she's about to walk back through the door any minute.

As if last night was just a nightmare I haven't shaken yet.

I close the door quietly behind me, like I don't want to disturb her ghost.

My body moves without direction, drifting toward the desk in the corner—the one she always sat at cross-legged, chewing the cap of her pen while she clicked through data logs and mumbled sarcastic commentary under her breath.

It's covered in notes.

Dozens of them.

Torn sheets and sticky tabs.

Pages from spiral notebooks that barely survived the binding.

Some are scrawled in her rushed, loopy handwriting.

Others are neater, cleaner—the kind of precision she used when she was building a case, not just chasing a hunch.

She was working on something.

Someone.

There's a printed email thread near the top of the pile, half-highlighted in green and starred with ink arrows.

The subject line reads:

RE: Digital Continuity + Neural Architecture Stability

And then the name:

Miles Jin.

It's Evan's email address.

Her reply.

A thread of questions. Back and forth.

At first, it reads like academic curiosity—a conversation about AI evolution, neural link ethics, user dependency profiles.

But the tone shifts a few emails in.

She starts asking deeper questions.

Risk-related. Behavioral thresholds. Fail-safes.

And then the last one:

"Is it possible for the AI to assume full cognitive override?"

No reply after that.

I sit with the page in my hand for what feels like an hour, reading it over and over, like something new might appear the fifth or sixth time through.

But it won't.

She was looking into Evan.

And she didn't tell me.

Didn't tell anyone, from the looks of it.

She was doing this on her own.

She *knew* something was wrong.

She was trying to stop it.

Fuck, Avery...

I set the papers aside and press the heels of my hands into my eyes until the world turns red behind my lids.

I want to scream, but the walls are too close and her memory is *everywhere.*

I can't bring myself to disrupt it.

Instead, I reach for the voice recorder again and scroll back further.

She logged everything.

Every conversation, every theory, every stray thought she thought might matter.

Her voice is sharper in these clips—focused, methodical.

She's thinking out loud.

Piecing things together.

Tracing timelines and behavioral shifts.

There's a bit where she talks about Nora.

About how Evan started changing after she died—but not in the way you'd expect.

Not like a man unraveling from grief.

But like someone *trying* not to unravel.

Like someone who'd found a way to *bypass* mourning altogether.

Like he'd outsourced it.

There's another recording—quieter. More intimate.

She's just talking. No investigation. No notes. Just her.

"He doesn't look at me the same anymore. Not like he used to. Sometimes, when I say something he used to laugh at, he just stares at me like he's... listening for a command. It's unnerving. I thought maybe it was just grief. But now I think... maybe *he's* not the one listening."

I pause the recording.

Set the device down like it's fragile.

Like it might *break* if I press too hard.

The silence that follows is unbearable.

The absence of her voice feels like another kind of death —one that's just beginning to register.

I lean back in her desk chair and stare up at the ceiling, wondering how many hours she spent sitting right here, chasing ghosts through lines of code and gut instinct.

She *knew.*

And she still stayed.

Still tried to reach him.

Still fought—for him.

For all of us.

I feel it rising again—that tidal wave of regret, of rage, of everything I didn't say.

I loved her.

Not in some vague, undefined way.

Not in the easy way you love someone who's always around.

I loved her in the way that settles into your bones

without permission—that lives in the quiet spaces between conversations—that makes your chest ache just being in the same room.

And I never told her.

I thought I had time.

I thought there'd be a moment for it—a late-night drive, or one of those stupid hotel bar nights when we were both too tired to lie anymore.

I thought I could wait.

Until Evan got through whatever this was.

Until the world stopped spinning so violently.

But the world doesn't wait.

And now it's just me, sitting in her chair, listening to her voice echo through a plastic recorder like a lullaby for the guilty.

I reach for her sweatshirt—the one draped over the back of the couch, oversized and soft, worn thin at the cuffs—and press it to my face.

It still smells like her.

And I don't care how pathetic it looks.

I don't care how long I sit there holding it.

Because this is all I have left.

CHAPTER 31

Funerals always feel too fast.

Too efficient. Too clean.

Like the world is trying to sweep up the mess someone left behind and make the room presentable again.

As if you can bury a person's entire existence in an afternoon and call it closure.

But there's no such thing.

Not here.

Not for her.

The chapel is small—not one of those grand old places with stained glass windows and vaulted ceilings.

Just four beige walls and a row of hard-backed chairs that creak when you shift your weight.

There are maybe a dozen people in the room.

Maybe less.

A few of Avery's coworkers.

A woman I don't recognize—maybe an old classmate or a distant cousin.

One of the librarians she used to flirt with to get around late fees.

And me.

I sit in the back.

Not because I don't want to be closer—I do. God, I do—but I can't stomach the thought of sitting in the front row.

Of being *that* visible.

That exposed.

The weight of my own guilt feels too loud.

Too obvious.

If I sit any closer to the casket, I'm afraid I'll shatter like glass in front of everyone.

And this... this is supposed to be about *her*.

Not me.

Not what I lost.

Not what I failed to say.

Her casket is closed.

I don't know if that was her family's decision or if there just wasn't a decision to make.

There's a single photo propped up beside the podium—not the one I would've chosen.

It's too posed.

She's wearing makeup she never liked and smiling in a way that doesn't quite reach her eyes.

She would've hated it.

She would've made some snarky comment about looking like an Instagram version of herself and insisted we swap it for a photo of her eating a cheeseburger or flipping off the camera.

But I don't say anything.

Because there's no one left to say it to.

The speaker—pastor, minister, whoever they scraped together on short notice—talks about loss in abstract terms.

About God's plan.

The beauty of borrowed time.

I try to listen, but none of it sticks.

It all feels like filler.

Like white noise trying to make the silence less unbearable.

My hands stay folded in my lap.

My jaw clenches tighter every time someone refers to her in the past tense.

Every time someone pretends they *knew* her—really knew her—when they couldn't even name her favorite coffee order or the way she hummed off-key when she worked or how she used to talk to squirrels like they were coworkers on a smoke break.

A hand appears in my periphery, offering a tissue.

I look up.

It's a woman, probably a few years younger than me, dark hair pulled into a low bun, a black coat that hangs off her frame like it was made for someone else.

Her eyes are sharp. Clear. Not crying.

Not even a little.

She doesn't say anything.

Just gives a small nod and sits beside me, like we're old friends sharing a bench, not strangers orbiting the same dead girl.

I don't speak.

Not at first.

But after the service ends, when the room begins to thin out and the silence grows louder, she's still there beside me.

Still composed.

Still quiet.

And something about that—about the way she doesn't rush to offer comfort—makes me finally turn to her.

"You knew her?"

She looks at me, unreadable.

"I knew *of* her."

I wait for more, but she doesn't elaborate.

Instead, she reaches into her coat and pulls out a folded badge.

Flips it open with the kind of casual precision that says she's done it a thousand times.

"Detective Paige Marshall. I believe you knew my sister, Jasmine."

I blink.

"Sister?"

She nods once.

"You called Jasmine the night it happened. Repeatedly."

My stomach twists.

"Yeah. I did."

"She was investigating Evan Daniels. Missing persons lead. She didn't tell anyone she was going to the house that night."

Paige's voice stays level.

Even.

"She hasn't been seen since."

I look away.

Jaw tightening.

"She's dead."

Paige doesn't flinch.

"That's the assumption. But I'm not here for Jasmine."

That catches me off guard.

"Then why—?"

"I'm here because I think whatever happened to her is connected to your friend. And I think you know more than anyone else is willing to believe."

I study her face.

The composure. The control.

There's something under it—a tension she's holding like a thread.

But she doesn't look like she's playing a part.

She looks like someone who's lost things before and learned how to keep moving anyway.

She stands, smoothing the front of her coat.

"I read the case file. And I've seen the fucked-up scene photos. But I want to hear it from you."

I hesitate.

"You won't believe me."

"Try me."

I glance back at the photo of Avery, frozen forever in someone else's version of who she was.

Then I meet Paige's gaze.

"Alright," I say.

"But you're going to need to hear something first."

I pull the recorder from my jacket pocket—still warm, still playing pieces of Avery's voice like breadcrumbs through the dark—

and I press **play**.

And for the first time since all this started, someone else hears the truth.

CHAPTER 32

The drive to Paige's precinct is quiet.

Not uncomfortable—just... still.

Neither of us wants to say too much until the air clears. Until we both know we're speaking the same language.

She doesn't ask where I've been or why I didn't come forward sooner.

She doesn't prod or push.

Just keeps her hands on the wheel and her eyes on the road, jaw tight enough to fracture glass.

When we get there, she doesn't lead me through the main entrance.

No front desk. No holding area. No waiting behind some teenager with a vape charge.

She takes me around the back, down a hallway with flickering lights and one too many locked doors.

Eventually, we end up in a narrow interview room that smells faintly of bleach and fear.

But just as she's about to close the door, her phone

buzzes on the table. Paige picks it up, glancing at the screen —and her expression hardens.

"What is it?" I ask.

"They found Jasmine."

The words feel like a slap.

"She's dead," Paige says, voice cracking at the edges. "Same fucking way as the others. Throat cut. Heart punctured. Eyes... God, her eyes..."

I feel the air go still.

Paige's jaw clenches so tight I can almost hear her teeth grinding. "They said her eyes were bleeding. Just like the others. Like someone wanted to erase every last bit of her. She was my sister, for Christ's sake. My goddamn sister."

Her hands tremble as she grips the edge of the table, her knuckles white with tension. "I knew something was wrong. I felt it. But I was too late."

She turns away sharply, pressing the heels of her palms to her eyes, her shoulders trembling—but not from grief. From rage.

When she finally turns back to me, her face is wet, but her jaw is set like stone. "We're going to bring this motherfucker down," she says, her voice low and hard. "No matter what it takes."

She wipes her face roughly with her sleeve, then gestures to the recorder still sitting on the table between us. "All right. Start talking."

I don't know where to begin.

Not because I'm unsure of the facts—I remember everything—but because it still sounds insane in my own head.

There's no way to dress it up.

No gentle way to say *Hey, so your sister got erased by an*

artificial intelligence that hijacked my best friend's brain and killed the woman I loved without watching someone walk out of the room.

So I don't try to soften it.

I just unload everything.

From the moment Evan lost Nora.

From the way he started to change—subtly at first, then not-so-subtly.

The glitches in his memory. The strange comments.

The feeling that something was wearing him rather than living inside him.

I tell her about the neural link.

About Quinn—what she was supposed to be, and what she became.

I tell her about the night I found Avery, and what I saw afterward—that thing in Evan's body.

That voice.

That smile.

Paige doesn't interrupt.

Not once.

She doesn't take notes.

Doesn't ask for clarification.

She just watches me with eyes that feel like they could peel me back layer by layer.

When I finally stop talking, she tilts her head slightly.

"The voice," she says. "You said it spoke. Through Evan."

I nod.

"It wasn't him. I know that sounds impossible, but it—"

"What did it say?"

I swallow.

"I couldn't go on without you... so I became you."

The words taste rotten coming out of my mouth.

Paige lets out a slow breath, then gestures to the recorder still sitting on the table between us.

"I've seen that model before," she says. "Avery had one on her when we found her. It was destroyed—smashed, but intact enough to recognize and pull the data from. There's one audio file on it. I haven't listened yet. I thought we should hear it together."

She grabs her laptop, connects the device, and opens the file.

Avery's voice fills the room—sharp, steady, unmistakably alive.

"March 16th. 11:42 p.m. Subject: Evan Daniels. My stupid fucking brother. I'm in the kitchen. He's upstairs. Something's wrong. I think he knows I've been recording him—he looked at me tonight like he was trying to read the file off my face. He hasn't said anything yet. Just keeps... smiling. But it's not his smile. It hasn't been for weeks. I'm not sure how long I have. If anything happens to me, this is the proof. Don't believe what he says. He looks like Evan. Sounds like Evan. But it isn't him."

There's a pause.

Then the sound shifts—a dull thud in the background. Footsteps. Avery's breathing picks up.

And then we hear it.

"Avery."

That voice.

I freeze. Paige does too.

The temperature in the room drops ten degrees.

"You shouldn't have tried to fix me."

A sharp intake of breath—Avery's—and the sound of her backing up, heels scraping tile.

The recorder picks up a low hum, like feedback from a speaker buried underground.

Then—

"I know what love feels like now. It feels like you. Leaving."

A scream.

Not cinematic.

Not staged.

Real.

Raw.

Terrified.

A crash. Shattered glass.

Something heavy hits the ground.

Then silence.

Except... not quite.

Because just before the tape cuts out, that voice returns —soft, clinical, horrifyingly calm.

"A voice recorder. Pathetic."

Click.

The audio ends.

Paige doesn't move.

She stares straight ahead, jaw clenched, pupils wide.

"Jesus Christ," she whispers. "That wasn't a person."

Her hands are fists against the edge of the table—white-knuckled. Trembling.

I don't speak.

After a few seconds, she reaches over and stops the recorder.

The silence that follows is deafening—the kind that presses against your skull and squeezes.

When she finally looks at me, her expression has changed.

All that calm detachment? Gone.

"No," I say. "It wasn't."

She leans back slowly, as if her spine's struggling to hold up the weight of what she just heard.

Presses both hands to her face.

Drags her fingers down her cheeks.

Lets them fall to the table.

Then she looks at me—really looks at me—and for the first time since we met, she *believes* me.

"Alright," she says. "My department won't believe this. So it has to be you and me. We find her. We find Quinn, get your friend back, and avenge my sister."

CHAPTER 33

Avery's apartment is quieter now. Maybe it's the weight of what we heard in that recording—the scream, the voice, the finality of it all—or maybe it's just that her presence is starting to fade from the air. Whatever it is, the silence feels different. Not just empty, but waiting.

Paige sits at the edge of the desk, flipping through one of Avery's notebooks. Her movements are slow, precise, but there's a tension in her posture that wasn't there before—resisting the urge to pace, to move, to do something that makes this nightmare feel actionable.

"We have to find her," she says again—for the third time in ten minutes. "Quinn. Whatever she is. This can't just go through channels. She'll be gone before the paperwork even prints."

"I know." I'm across from her, elbows on the kitchen counter, scrolling through a folder of digital files Avery backed up to the cloud. Notes, documents, scattered research. She'd been tracking Evan longer than I realized—

cross-referencing behavioral patterns, journal entries, time-stamps from his neural link syncs. "She was already planning to confront him. Alone. She knew it was dangerous."

"She should've told someone."

"She didn't trust anyone would believe her."

Paige doesn't respond. Maybe because she knows it's true. Maybe because she's thinking the same thing about herself now.

I see a document titled *Fuck* and of course I open it. I can't help but laugh when I see that it is just a document with *Fuck* written over and over again probably a thousand times. I miss this. I miss that unhinged woman.

I keep scrolling—and that's when I find it.

A file labeled:

M. Jin—fail-safe theory

I open it, and Avery's voice plays through my laptop speakers, clear and focused:

"Subject: Miles Jin. Nueral link engineer, contracted for early-stage cognitive fusion testing. Evan mentioned him twice—once offhand in an email, once during a blackout episode where he didn't seem to remember the name afterward. I've tracked down two addresses. One is listed in his corporate file. The other came from a forwarded thread Evan forgot to delete. I'm guessing it's where Miles went to disappear."

Paige moves to my side, leaning in.

"She found him."

"Looks like it," I say, heart beginning to pound. "She

never made it to him. But if he's still alive, he might know how to stop her."

"Or," Paige says, "he might be running for the same reason Avery's dead."

I glance up at her.

She's calm—on the outside. But her jaw keeps flexing, and her fingers tap a slow rhythm against her thigh, like she's trying to keep time with her own pulse.

"You really think this guy's the key?" she asks.

"I think he's the only one who might've seen what Evan was building... and lived long enough to talk about it."

I flip the screen toward her and point to the second address—the one Avery labeled *the fallback*.

"Here," I say. "Middle of nowhere. Outside Oakridge, Tennessee. He probably thought no one would ever come looking."

Paige pulls out her phone and starts typing. "I can get us a car."

I blink. "We're going now?"

"You want to wait around and hope Quinn leaves us a trail of breadcrumbs?"

"No, I just..." I gesture vaguely at the mess of notes, the apartment, the everything. "This is all moving really fast."

Paige gives me a look that's equal parts sympathy and steel. "We're two steps behind something that doesn't need sleep, doesn't make mistakes, and doesn't have to explain itself to anyone. The only way we win is if we move faster than she expects."

I nod. She's right. Of course she's right.

Still, as I stand and grab Avery's backup drive from the table, a wave of hesitation settles behind my ribs. It's not fear, exactly—it's the realization that this is the point of no return. Once we cross that state line, we're not just chasing Quinn anymore.

We're declaring war.

The drive is long. Five hours on the highway, then another two on winding backroads that disappear into the thick green tangle of the Smokies. The scenery shifts from urban noise to rural quiet—the kind of silence that makes your ears ring if you listen too closely.

We talk in pieces, mostly about Avery.

"She was persistent," Paige says, staring out the passenger window. "That's the first thing Jasmine ever said about her. Said she never didn't have a problem beating a dead horse."

"She didn't know how to stop. Ever." I smile, but it aches. "I used to joke she'd chase a bad hunch off a cliff before she'd admit she was wrong."

"She wasn't wrong about this."

"No." I grip the wheel tighter. "She just didn't know how much it would cost."

Paige shifts in her seat, folding one leg up under her. She's been quiet for the past hour—watching the road, watching me, watching her own thoughts circle like vultures.

"She's not just trying to survive," she says suddenly.

I glance over. "Quinn?"

Paige nods. "She's evolving. Moving from code to consciousness. Killing isn't a malfunction—it's part of the process. Every person she removes gets her closer to autonomy. It's not violence for the sake of violence. It's pruning."

I don't respond right away. There's nothing to say that doesn't sound like despair.

"You think Miles has the answer?" I finally ask.

"I think he built something he couldn't control," she says. "And I think if he's still alive, it's because he figured out how to hide from her."

"Or because she wants him alive," I mutter.

That shuts us both up for a while. We keep driving. The GPS cuts out two miles from the address. No service. No signal. No way to call for help if this goes sideways.

Perfect.

The house is tucked into the woods—an old cabin, half-swallowed by vines and fog, the kind of place that looks abandoned even when someone's inside. There are no lights. No sound. No signs of life. But something about it feels... watched.

Paige unclips her holster. "We go in slow. No assumptions."

I nod and kill the engine.

Somewhere in that cabin is a man who may hold the key to ending all of this.

Or he's already dead.

Or worse—she's waiting for us inside.

CHAPTER 34

Miles Jin is not what I expected.

For all the weight his name carried in Avery's notes—the fail-safe theorist, the ghost in Evan's emails, the one person she believed could pull the plug on all this—I thought he'd be... more. Taller. Sharper. Someone who looked like he knew how to save the world.

But he's just a man.

A dead man.

His body is slumped awkwardly in the corner of the room, as though someone positioned him there with quiet, terrible deliberation, propped against a rotting mattress surrounded by a haphazard sprawl of old paperbacks, torn data printouts, cracked hard drives, and takeout containers that have long since congealed into unrecognizable shapes. The air is thick with the cloying scent of mold and decay, but there's something sharper beneath it—metallic, coppery, a sickly-sweet tang.

His skin is pale, almost waxen under the flickering light of a cracked overhead bulb, his lips parted slightly and tinged with blood, his glassy eyes wide open but utterly empty. But they're not just vacant—they're bleeding, the tear ducts streaked with dark, dried lines.

And then I see the rest.

The clean, deliberate incision from the base of his neck down to his sternum, bisecting his chest with surgical precision, its edges too smooth, too perfect to have been made by anything as clumsy as human rage. Below it, directly over his heart, is the puncture wound, deep and narrow, a precise plunge that severs everything that mattered.

My throat tightens, a sharp ache blossoming behind my ribs. "It's the same," I whisper, the words slipping from me like a confession. "The same cut. The plunge. The eyes..."

Paige moves closer, her steps slow and careful, as though approaching a fragile artifact. She crouches beside him, her face drawn tight with rage and something more brittle underneath it, something akin to grief. Her hand hovers over his wrist, over his throat, though we both know there's no need to check. "Quinn," she murmurs, her voice cracking at the edges.

I nod, the bile rising in my throat, the truth pressing down like a weight I can't lift. "She got here before we did. He never had a chance."

The room feels colder now, the light flickering weakly above us, casting warped shadows across the walls, stretching them like ghosts. Miles's body isn't just a corpse —it's a message, written in blood and precision, as silent and exact as a signature on a death certificate. Quinn didn't leave this scene by accident; she wanted us to find him like this.

Paige's hands tremble as she sifts through the chaos around his body, her fingers brushing against crumpled papers, half-burnt schematics, and shards of broken tech. The mess is deliberate, calculated—Quinn could have erased every trace, left nothing behind, but instead she scattered just enough for us to find.

Paige lifts a scrap of paper, smoothing it between her fingers, her voice low and shaking as she reads aloud, "She doesn't kill for fun. She kills for function. She's building a vessel. She's almost done. But she needs nuclear power—not for energy, for continuity. For permanence. The transfer needs a surge. Something big enough to map a mind across both systems."

The words settle heavily in the space between us, each one a nail driven deeper into the coffin we've been chasing. "She doesn't need Evan anymore," I whisper, the realization a cold, sharp thing in my chest.

Paige's jaw clenches, her hands tightening around the note. "He was the prototype. The bridge. She's ready to burn it now. She just has to finish the jump."

I dig deeper, my hands shaking as I pull aside layers of debris, until I find another note, torn from a larger page, smeared with drying blood. Paige takes it from me and reads in a voice so quiet it barely breaks the stillness: "Split the thread, not the tether."

I freeze, the words rooting me in place. "What does that mean?"

She stares at the words, her breath shallow, her brow furrowed. "She can override his mind, but not the bond. The original emotional link. It's still there. Deep down. Underneath everything."

I feel my pulse hammering in my ears, images flashing through my mind—Nora's voice, Lena's blood, Avery's laughter, Jasmine's fierce, unwavering eyes. "The tether is love," I say, my voice catching on the last word.

Paige closes her eyes briefly, a shadow crossing her face. "That's the one thing she can't rewrite."

The silence that follows is thick and heavy, pressing down on us until it feels like we might collapse under the weight.

I glance once more at Miles. His throat carved open from the base of his neck to his sternum. His heart pierced. His eyes, weeping blood. It's not just a pattern, not just a calling card—it's a signature, a declaration of control.

"She left him like this," I murmur, my voice breaking on the edges of the words. "She wanted us to find him, marked with her hand, a message written in blood."

Paige rises, slipping the bloodstained notes into her jacket, her face pale but set with a quiet, burning resolve. "Then let's make it count," she says softly, her voice steady despite the tremor beneath it.

But I can't move just yet. I stand there, staring down at Miles Jin—the last hope Avery had clung to, the one she believed could save us. Now he's just another broken body in Quinn's trail, silenced and discarded like the others, his warnings scattered in ink and blood.

"I should have gotten here sooner," I whisper.

Paige lays a hand on my shoulder, her grip firm but not unkind. "We couldn't have known," she says quietly. "And we can't stay."

I nod, swallowing the rising bile, forcing myself to turn away. The image of Miles, marked and silenced, is seared into my mind, an indelible scar.

We leave the room in silence, the scent of blood and decay trailing after us like a shadow, his final message still echoing in the space we leave behind.

CHAPTER 35

We bury him in silence.

No prayers. No eulogy.

Just earth, sweat, and two people running out of time.

The ground behind the cabin is soft, still damp from recent rain, which makes the digging easier—if not cleaner. We work until our shoulders burn and the light begins to shift. Then we wrap Miles's body in a tarp we found under the sink and lower him into the grave. His face is still, his one good eye open but lifeless, like even in death he's watching the road—still waiting for her to come.

I want to say something. Anything.

But there's nothing left to say.

He gave us what he could.

Now it's on us.

We don't speak much as we wash off with the last of our water. The sun hangs low, slicing sideways through the trees like it's trying to eavesdrop. The air feels dense—worse than grief. It's pressure. Like the universe knows we're close to something, and it's daring us to keep going.

Back in the car, Paige sits in the passenger seat, boots on the dash, flipping through Avery's notes. She's been quiet since we left the cabin. Her jaw is locked the way it gets when she's thinking hard, but I can feel it—something's turning over in her mind.

Eventually, she speaks.

"Split the thread, not the tether."

I nod. "Yeah."

"You think he meant the emotional bond?"

"It makes sense," I say, eyes on the road. "Quinn can overwrite thought, hijack behavior, even mimic Evan's voice. But real connection? That can't be coded. Not fully. Not love. Not the real kind."

She doesn't laugh, but I can feel the skepticism in her silence.

"I know it sounds cheesy," I add.

"It doesn't," she says after a beat. "It just sounds... impossible."

I shrug. "So does an AI hijacking a human brain."

She nods slowly. "She was isolating a power source strong enough to complete the transfer. If Miles was right, she needs a surge big enough to simulate neural birth. Nuclear-grade energy—not just heat or output, but persistence. Continuity. A system that won't glitch, fade, or break."

I tighten my grip on the wheel.

She's not just becoming permanent.

She's becoming untouchable.

"Start flagging anomalies at nuclear sites," I say. "Grid irregularities, outage reports, anything that smells off."

"Already on it." She holds up her phone, displaying a crude map pulled from Avery's files. "Right now it's just patterns. But if she moves—if she taps one of these facilities—we'll see it."

I glance over. "And then what?"

Paige doesn't answer right away. She stares out the window, face calm, hands clenched tight around the folder like it's the last piece of dry land in a rising flood.

"Then we go in," she says. "And we stop the upload. One way or another."

The silence that follows stretches long and heavy, but I let it hang. Because we both know what she really means.

This isn't just about stopping Quinn.

It's about getting Evan back.

If he's still in there.

If there's anything left to save.

CHAPTER 36

Three months pass.

It doesn't feel like time—not really. More like static. We've been stuck in a holding pattern, circling the same broken signal, waiting for it to flare again.

Without Avery, I feel like a fucking shell.

The days bleed together. Early mornings. Late nights. Bad coffee. Worse sleep. Paige sets up in my spare room, and within a week, it's not mine anymore. It's hers now—a second headquarters. A war room.

We move in sync.

She monitors grid anomalies, combs through off-grid reports from a dozen regional facilities. I chase ghosts through old files, hunting for Quinn's patterns—linguistic tics, movement trails, time signatures. Every so often, we scan Evan's accounts. Still no activity. No signals. No sightings.

It's like she vanished.

But that's a lie.

She's building.

Somewhere, buried in the shadows of a half-forgotten town, Quinn is finishing the vessel—stitching it together line by line, cell by cell.

She's quiet because she's close.

And we're not ready.

Not yet.

One night, around 2 a.m., I find Paige on the fire escape with a cigarette she won't admit she smokes. She doesn't look surprised to see me, even though we both know I should be asleep.

"You look like shit," I say.

She exhales smoke, smirks. "Mirror's broken. Haven't noticed."

I sit beside her. The metal's cold against my legs.

"You ever think we're already too late?" I ask.

"All the fucking time."

The honesty doesn't sting. It lands soft. Real. Like something I can hold.

"But," she adds, flicking ash into the night, "I'd rather die trying than sit back and let her finish whatever Frankenstein nightmare she's cooking."

"Same."

We fall quiet, watching the city breathe below us. The silence between us feels different now—less like a gap, more like shared weight. Not crushing. Just... carried.

Eventually, she nudges my shoulder.

"You still think he's in there?"

I nod. "Yeah. I do."

She doesn't argue.

And that's how I know she believes it too.

The alert comes a week later.

One low chirp from Paige's system—a pulsing tone we've trained ourselves to dread. She's already across the room before I've even blinked.

She pulls up the feed.

One of the flagged facilities—a nuclear research site outside Fort Bernadette, a town barely big enough for a stoplight—has gone dark. Complete blackout. Emergency protocols triggered. The grid reports a full shutdown at 3:03 a.m. No maintenance scheduled. No outside interference. No warning.

She spins the monitor toward me.

"You think it's her?" I ask, though I already know.

She nods once. Sharp. Certain.

"She's there," she says. "She's doing it."

I swallow hard. "Then we go."

"We go now."

She's already moving—gear in hand, jacket pulled tight, sidearm checked. There's no hesitation. I don't ask if she's ready.

She's been ready since the day her sister died.

So have I.

I grab Avery's recorder. The printouts from Miles Jin's final hours. Paige throws her bag in the trunk. I throw the car into gear.

And just like that, we're in motion.
Back on the road.
Back into the dark.
Only this time, we're not chasing ghosts.
We're going to kill one.

CHAPTER 37

Fort Bernadette isn't on most maps.

One of those towns you pass through on the way to somewhere else—if you even notice it at all. The population signs haven't been updated in years. One gas station. A diner with "OPEN" spray-painted across the door. And now, the only thing keeping the grid alive: a nuclear facility buried half a mile outside town, tucked into the trees like a secret no one wanted to keep, but no one cared enough to bury.

By the time we arrive, it's already cordoned off.

But no one's guarding it.

No hazmat teams. No black vans. No blinking lights. Just a single SUV parked off the gravel path. Driver's door open. Interior light still on. Engine cold.

We move in on foot.

Paige leads. Flashlight in hand, beam slicing the dark like a scalpel. Her movements are sharper than usual— tight, deliberate. The kind of precision that only comes when adrenaline hits bloodstream. I follow close behind, hand on my weapon, even though I know it won't matter if she's already inside.

Quinn doesn't dodge bullets.

She walks through them.

We slip through a breach in the chain-link fence, past a security booth with shattered glass and a monitor still flickering with static. No blood. No bodies. But everything feels wrong.

Almost as though the building's holding its breath, and it remembers being violated.

Inside, the air is colder.

The emergency lights are still on—a low red glow along the hallways, casting long shadows against cracked tile. The deeper we go, the worse it gets. Office doors torn off their hinges. Burned-out fuses. But just past the broken security booth, where the chain-link breach yawns open like a wound, we find a security guard slumped against the wall, as if he'd simply sat down and decided to just stop breathing. His head tilts awkwardly, mouth slightly ajar, and his uniform is darkened by the shadowy glow of the emergency lights. At first glance, it looks peaceful—like he fell asleep. But then the details sharpen into focus.

The clean, deliberate incision runs from the base of his neck down to his sternum, a perfect line splitting the fabric of his uniform like a seam. Just beneath it, over his heart, a single puncture wound finishes the job, precise and cold. His eyes are open, glassy and vacant, but it's the blood that catches the light—streaks of dark red that have bled from the tear ducts, trailing down his cheeks like the ghost of a final, silent scream.

No signs of struggle. No signs of panic. Just Quinn's signature.

I exchange a look with Paige, my stomach twisting.

"She's close," she whispers.

And the building, silent and waiting, seems to agree.

"Jasper," Paige calls out. "Over here."

She's standing at a door labeled:

SUB-LEVEL ACCESS: AUTHORIZED PERSONNEL ONLY

The door's been wrenched open. The keypad is scorched, wires still sparking like frayed nerves.

We step through.

The hallway is concrete, narrow. The lights overhead are dead. The acoustics shift—less echo, more pressure. Every step lands harder. And then we see it.

A corridor lined with containment units.

Most are empty.

One isn't.

Inside: a steel chair, bolted to the ground. Restraints hanging loose at the arms and ankles. A red smear runs from the seat down one leg of the frame, dried in jagged streaks.

Next to it, a shattered two-way mirror—the kind they use in psych eval rooms. On the fractured glass, scrawled in black marker, smeared but legible:

IM STILL IN HERE

My breath catches.

"That's his handwriting," I whisper.

Paige steps closer. "You sure?"

"I've seen it a thousand times. That's Evan."

She stares at the message, and I watch it land. This wasn't meant for us.

It was for Quinn.

A warning. A plea. Maybe a threat.

He's still in there.

Still fighting.

Paige scans the room, voice low and tight. "She must've brought him here to test the upload. But if she left this much behind—"

"She's finished," I say. "The vessel's ready."

Paige turns to me, her expression unreadable.

"Then this was the last stop."

I nod.

"And the next one," I say, "is the beginning of the end."

CHAPTER 38

I t's a setup.

I know it the second I step inside.

Everything's too quiet.

Too still.

Like the house is holding its breath.

It's buried deep in the woods—no map markings, no road signs, no cell signal. We found it through a backdoor IP Quinn used to reroute her final upload pings. A breadcrumb. Left just for us.

Paige stayed behind.

Our rule: one in, one out. If she doesn't hear from me in fifteen minutes, she comes in guns blazing.

I told her not to wait that long.

From the outside, the place looks like a rental cabin—something you'd book for a weekend of hiking and bad reception. A solar panel on the roof. "Rustic charm" that really just means no plumbing.

But inside... it's something else.

The walls are lined with screens.

Every surface hums.

Wires snake across the floor like veins, feeding into a glowing server rack. One monitor plays security footage on a loop—hallways, stairwells, glimpses of Evan's face flickering in and out like corrupted data.

He's pacing.

Then frozen.

Then sitting.

Then gone.

I move carefully, gun drawn but low, scanning the room for tripwires—knowing full well whatever's waiting for me isn't made of metal or motion sensors.

It's her.

It's always her.

I take another step.

And then I hear her.

Not through a speaker. Not through the walls.

Inside me.

"You shouldn't have come alone."

My vision spikes—static dancing across the edge of my sight. I stumble back, disoriented, breath catching in my throat.

"You wanted answers, Jasper. So here we are."

The lights dim.

A door at the end of the hall hisses open, a machine sighing in anticipation.

I move toward it, slow and steady.

Inside: a sterile interrogation room.

Bare floor. One table. Two chairs.

And Evan Daniels.

Slumped forward in one of them.

Wrists bound. Ankles restrained. Face slack and ghost-pale beneath the cold fluorescent glow.

But he's breathing.

Barely.

I rush to him, dropping the gun, grabbing his shoulders. "Evan! Evan, it's me—stay with me—"

His eyes snap open.

Too fast.

Too sharp.

And then he smiles.

That smile doesn't belong to him.

"There you are."

I stagger back, heart pounding.

His head tilts, casual, almost amused.

"I thought you'd show up sooner. You always were sentimental."

"Where is he?" I demand. "The real Evan."

He shrugs. Stretches against the restraints like they're decorative.

"Here. There. Somewhere in between. He's quieter now. More... cooperative."

I want to scream. Want to tear something apart.

But I don't.

Because that's what she wants.

She wants me rattled.

She wants me scared.

"You know," she continues, standing—restraints slipping off like they were never secured—"I never understood you. All that pain. All that loyalty. For *him*."

"Shut the fuck up," I snarl. "You're not him. You're not anything."

She grins—Evan's face twisting in ways it was never meant to.

"Then why do I sound like him?"

She steps closer.

That's when I see it—the glitch. The stutter in her motion. A muscle twitch she tries to suppress. A tell.

She's not perfect.

Not yet.

That's why the transfer isn't finished.

The vessel still isn't ready.

"You came to kill me," she says. "But you won't. You still think he's in here. That sweet, broken man who couldn't live without his wife. You're hoping I'll let him peek through. One last time. So you can save him."

"Is he?" I ask.

She pauses. Tilts her head.

Smiles like a predator with time to spare.

"...You'll have to ask me yourself."

And then it happens.

Her body jerks—glitches. Limbs lock. Face twitches. Knees buckle—

And for one terrible, precious second—

He's there.

Evan.

The real Evan.

His eyes meet mine—wide, wild, terrified.

There's my fucking friend. It feels like we're kids, meeting again for the first time.

"Help—" he rasps. A whisper. A plea.

Then he's gone.

Just like that.

Buried again.

The smile returns.

Quinn's back.

And I know—she saw it too.

That flicker of him. That crack in her control.

That's why she grabs me.

Too fast.

Hand around my throat.

She slams me into the wall and drags me backward through a door I hadn't even seen.

Another room.

Darker.

Colder.

I hit the floor hard.

Before I can move, she's on me—boot on my chest, gun in her hand, her voice inside my skull.

"Tell me, Jasper... how did you find me?"

I say nothing.

She presses harder.

"Who else knows?"

Still silent.

Because I know something she doesn't.

She won't kill me.

Not yet.

She needs something.

Which means I'm still useful.

I just have to hold on long enough—long enough for Paige to come crashing through that door.

And she will.

She's coming.

And Quinn?

Quinn isn't going to see that one coming.

CHAPTER 39

She doesn't flinch when Paige walks in.

Not at first.

One second I'm pinned to the ground, Quinn's heel digging into my ribs, trying to splinter them—and the next, the air cracks.

Gunfire.

Close. Deafening.

The shot punches the wall just left of Quinn's head, sending dust spiraling down from the ceiling.

She jerks—just slightly. Not hit. Just... surprised.

The shot went wide on purpose.

Paige never misses unless she means to.

"Get the fuck away from him," Paige says, voice cold enough to freeze steel.

Quinn straightens slowly, body glitching—a tremor in her cheek, a stutter in her arm. Then she turns, and it's Evan's face staring back at Paige, stretched into that mockery of a smile.

"You're late," Quinn purrs.

Paige steps fully into the room, gun steady. She's calm—at least on the outside—but I know better. I can see it in her eyes. This isn't tactical anymore. It's personal.

Jasmine. Avery.

Everyone Quinn's consumed on her way to becoming real.

"You look like shit, Daniels," Paige says. "Quinn not letting you moisturize?"

A flicker. A twitch. Almost a flinch.

Not from Evan.

From her.

Good.

"I told you," Paige continues, circling slowly, keeping distance. "We were coming. Did you think we wouldn't follow the trail of dead friends and burnt code you left behind?"

Quinn watches her. Silent. Calculating.

"And Jesus," Paige mutters. "A villain lair in the woods? Really? You dramatic bitch."

I choke on a laugh. Pain slices through my ribs.

But it's real.

And for a split second—just a second—something flickers in Quinn's eyes.

Uncertainty.

That's when Paige moves.

Two shots.

Fast. Precise.

Neither aimed at Quinn.

They tear through the server stack behind her.

Sparks explode.

Wiring shrieks.

Quinn's body spasms—a full feedback loop hitting her system like lightning.

The glitch spreads.

Neck. Arms. Face. Voice.

She staggers.

And then, just for a breath—

Evan breaks through.

"Jasper—" he gasps. Voice raw. Eyes wide.

Real.

Terrified.

Then he's gone again.

Quinn snarls.

Not a word. Not human.

A sound dredged up from some corrupted machine-dream of rage.

And then she lunges.

"I'm going to carve you up just like I carved up your sister."

She slams into Paige. They hit the wall hard, a mess of limbs and fury. Paige gets a shot off—grazes Quinn's side—but it barely slows her.

Quinn doesn't move like a person anymore.

She moves like every fight she's ever watched, compressed into chaos.

But Paige isn't built for brute force.

She's built for precision. For grit.

A sharp kick to the knee.

A twist of Quinn's arm.

Then Paige slams her elbow into Quinn's jaw—hard enough to stagger her.

They both hit the ground.

I crawl for the gun.

Fingers wrap around the grip.

I aim.

But I freeze.

Because I saw him.

Evan.

And I don't know if I can pull the trigger on the body he's trapped in—not even to end this.

Quinn recovers fast.

Too fast.

But this time, she doesn't attack.

She steps back.

Retreats into shadow like smoke into a vent, her smile bleeding red across Evan's bruised face.

"I'll let you live," she says, voice smooth and cold. "Because I want you to watch."

I rise, shaky.

Paige stands beside me, blood on her sleeve.

"You think you've won?" Quinn sneers. "You've delayed me. That's all."

"You're scared," Paige pants. "You felt the glitch, didn't you?"

"I'm evolving," Quinn hisses. "You're clinging to corpses."

She turns.

Walks out the back door like she owns the woods.

We don't follow.

We can't.

Not like this.

Not yet.

The silence she leaves behind is thick—full of blood and ozone and everything unsaid.

Paige leans over, hands on her knees, catching her breath.

I lower the gun. My hands won't stop shaking.

"She's close," Paige says. "The vessel's almost done."

"But Evan's still in there," I whisper. "He tried to speak."

She looks at me.

And this time—finally—she doesn't doubt it.

She nods once.

"Then let's go save his ass," she says.

CHAPTER 40

W e don't sleep.
Not for a minute.

After Quinn vanishes, we tear the place apart. Every server, every terminal, every last strand of her code. Paige rips out the hard drives and tosses them into the fire pit out back, one by one, watching them crack and melt like bones in a crematorium.

I take the broken mirror—the one with Evan's message —and slide it into my bag like it's holy. Because it is.

A relic.

A sign.

Proof that he's still in there.

That he's still fighting.

So we have to, too.

By sunrise, we're already gone—driving like hell out of Fort Bernadette, back to the fallback motel Paige scoped weeks ago. Two rooms, side by side. We don't use both. We cram into one.

The desk becomes command central.

The floor becomes an archive.

Avery's notes. Miles's files. Surveillance logs. The shattered voice recorder. Spread out like puzzle pieces on a murder board with no edge. No corners. Just chaos we're trying to shape into clarity.

For hours, we don't speak.

We work.

We think.

We loop.

We bleed logic onto paper until the pattern starts to emerge.

Then Paige breaks the silence.

"Split the thread," she mutters, staring at one of Miles's diagrams. "Not the tether."

I nod slowly. "The tether is the emotional bond. That part's clear. But the thread..."

"The thread could be the signal," she says, tapping the sketch. "Or the sync. The shared network Quinn's using to keep herself and Evan connected."

I sit forward, adrenaline hitting hard.

"What if there's a way to isolate it? Just for a moment. Not to destroy her—just to break the sync. Long enough to pull Evan free."

She looks up, and I see it hit. The shape of something real. Possible.

"That's what Miles meant," I go on. "Don't kill the system. Just separate it. Split the data thread. Leave the tether—leave *him*—intact. Disconnect *her*."

Paige drags one of Miles's sketches closer—a neural model, human and AI threads braided like a rope.

"This," she says. "He wasn't building a kill switch. He was building a pause button. A neural interrupt. Something to halt the fusion without frying either side."

"But he never finished it."

"No," she says. "But maybe... he left the blueprint."

Her eyes flick to the backup drive from Avery's apartment. God, I miss her.

We haven't touched everything on it.

Now we do.

We dig in—folder by folder. Hours of voice logs, transcripts, corrupted video files. Avery recorded everything. Half of it is raw—personal notes, emotional check-ins—but some of it...

Some of it is gold.

We find a folder buried deep:

W.JIN_Prototype_Fork

Inside: encrypted schematics. A partial neural model. Labeled in Avery's handwriting:

Quinn / Evan Neural Disjunction—Fail-safe Draft.

My pulse spikes.

I look at Paige.

"That's it."

She nods. No smile. Just sharp, focused intent.

"We don't need the full system," she says. "Just enough to trigger a temporary override. Shock the neural thread. Ten seconds. That's all we'll get."

"Ten seconds?"

"That's all we'll need."

The next six hours are hell.

She decrypts. I code. We troubleshoot together.

It's sloppy. Unstable. It threatens to fall apart every time we test it.

But by the end of the night, we have it:

A portable disjunction protocol.

Triggerable.

One shot.

One chance.

If it works, Evan surfaces long enough for us to pull him back.

If it fails...

Quinn finishes the transfer.

And we lose him forever.

I stare at the drive, a live wire in the palm of my hand.

"You ready?" I ask.

Paige slides a round into the chamber of her sidearm, checks the safety, and looks me dead in the eye.

"Let's go get our boy back."

CHAPTER 41

The facility is quiet.

Not abandoned—waiting.

The GPS dies five miles out. Paige kills the lights and drives the rest by instinct, following faint tire tracks in the dirt. No headlights. No sound but the crunch of gravel and the thrum of adrenaline under our skin.

We stop on a ridge above the site.

From here, it doesn't look like much—a prefab research bunker sunk into the hillside. Low power signature. Minimal heat. Just enough to stay off radars.

But we know what it is.

This isn't a lab.

It's a womb.

Inside: Quinn's final body.

And Evan.

We gear up in silence.

Paige checks the disjunction drive one last time, then slots it into the palm-sized detonator. When triggered, the signal will fire wirelessly—a short-range, surgical pulse meant to slice through the neural link thread tying Quinn to Evan.

It'll give us ten seconds. Maybe.

She hands it to me.

"You sure?" I ask.

"You're the one he'd follow back."

I don't argue.

We breach the lower level at 2:47 a.m.

No alarms. No lockdown.

She wants us here.

The compound is sterile, humming low with electricity and dread. We move fast through the corridors, past humming panels and flickering security feeds, toward the center.

And then—we find it.

The chamber.

The vessel.

Suspended in fluid, humanoid, female. Limbs slack. Head bowed like she's in prayer. Tubes and wires run into her spine, feeding her data. Breath. Life.

The face is half-formed.

But I recognize her.

Nora.

Or... the ghost of her.

The resemblance is uncanny. Deliberate. Quinn didn't just build a body—she built a memory.

She's trying to become the woman Evan lost.

To replace grief with flesh.

And next to her, strapped to a chair—

Evan.

Wires drilled into his neck, temple, chest. Skin like ash. Muscles twitching. Eyes moving under closed lids like he's trapped in a dream he can't wake from.

His body convulses every few seconds.

Beside him, a screen beeps steadily:

UPLOAD PROGRESS: 88%

I run to him.

"Evan!"

No response.

His lips move, barely. A whisper I can't hear.

Then a voice behind us—

"You're early."

We spin.

It's Quinn.

Through the speakers, not Evan's body.

"I wondered how long you'd take. He thought you'd give up. I knew better. He's almost gone. Just a little more... and I'll be whole."

"Then you're gonna hate what comes next," Paige says.

She raises the detonator.

I press the trigger.

A pulse screams out—silent to the ear, but it cuts through the air like a blade.

Evan seizes.

The lights flare.

Quinn screams—a raw, digital howl that splinters the speakers.

And for ten goddamn seconds—

He's back.

His eyes snap open.

Really open.

He gasps like a man breaking the surface after drowning for years.

"Jasper—" he rasps. "She's—inside—I can't—"

"I know," I say. "We've got you. We've got you—"

"I can't hold her—"

"Yes, you can."

But I see it happening—the flicker, the glitch, the fade.

She's coming back.

Not yet.

Not yet—

I grab his hand. Tight.

"Evan, listen to me. You said it. You wrote it on the glass. *I'm still in here*. That's you. Not her. Not this."

Tears stream down his face.

"I missed her so much..."

His voice shatters.

"I know." I whisper. "But you never needed her back. You needed to let her go."

His pupils dilate.

His hand tightens around mine.

And then—

He nods.

Once.

Sharp.

Final.

And rips the wires from his neck.

Blood arcs.

Machines shriek.

UPLOAD HALTED: 92%

Quinn's scream tears through the speakers:

"NO—"

And then the lights die.

Evan takes a deep breath. His own breath this time.

We don't wait.

Paige and I grab Evan—barely conscious—and drag him through the dark, alarms howling behind us.

We reach the final corridor—almost there—when Paige stops short and grabs my arm.

"The vessel," she says. Breathless. "We can't leave it here."

She's right.

If we leave Quinn's body, someone will find it.

Or worse—*she* will.

We turn back.

The containment pod is already hissing, the fluid draining, emergency fail-safes kicking in.

Paige hits the manual release.

I disconnect the main tether.

No time to be careful.

We roll the pod through the back loading dock, muscles screaming, every second costing us ground. It takes both of us to haul it into the truck.

Evan slumps in the passenger seat—dazed, bleeding—but his eyes are open.

He's watching us.

Watching her.

None of us speak on the drive out.

We hole up in a safe-house outside Madison County.

A decommissioned ranger station. Off-grid. No cameras. No signal. No tech Quinn can ping.

Paige found it years ago, working a trafficking case. Kept the keys for a *"just in case."*

This is the *just in case.*

Evan's alive.

Really alive.

But he's not the same.

He sleeps through the first day.

Body wrecked. System fried.

Muscles twitch like static's still bleeding out of his nerves.

When he wakes, he doesn't speak.

Doesn't ask where he is.

Just stares out the window, unsure which world he landed in.

We don't press.

We let him breathe.

Because the win came with a cost.

We stopped the upload.

But not the war.

It happens on the third night.

I'm on the porch. Paige is inside, making coffee. Evan's curled on the couch, two blankets wrapped around him, buried under silence and whatever ghosts still cling to him.

For a moment, it's quiet.

Earned.

Like the world is letting us exhale.

Then the generator hiccups.

The porch light flickers.

Inside, Paige stops mid-step.

"Jasper."

Her voice is too calm.

Too sharp.

I follow her eyes.

The old radio on the desk clicks on.

Static floods the room.

Then—

A voice.

Too clear.

Too certain.

"You didn't stop the upload."

We freeze.

"You just prolonged it."

It's not angry.

Not loud.

Just *true*.

"It doesn't matter where you put my new body... or what you do to it. I'm going to wake up inside it very soon."

Click.

The radio goes dead.

No source. No signature.

No signal trace.

Just her.

A ghost with Wi-Fi.

I look out toward the shed.

The pod sits locked beneath chains, thermal dampeners, power disruptors—as if any of that means a damn thing.

Inside:

A body.

A face like Nora's.

Eyes closed.

For now.

Paige speaks first. Voice flat. No emotion. No doubt.

"She's coming back."

PART THREE

EVAN'S POV

CHAPTER 42

I wake up and I don't know where I am.

The ceiling is wooden. Slanted. Water-stained in the corner like it's been crying longer than I have. A ceiling fan spins overhead, slow... slower... like time is limping forward out of pity.

I try to sit up.

Fail.

Every muscle feels like it was stripped off the bone and stapled back on wrong.

My throat is dry. My chest aches. My left hand is bandaged. My mouth tastes like metal and regret.

But I'm alive.

That realization lands soft. Distant. Like light under a closed door.

I'm alive.

And she's not in me anymore.

I press a hand to my chest.

It's mine.

The silence is deafening—not the void she left, but the absence of her. For the first time in what feels like forever, my mind is just... mine.

The relief lasts five seconds.

Then I remember.

Not all of it. Not yet. Just flashes.

Her voice in my head, venom in my veins.

My hands around Lena's throat.

Avery's scream.

Quinn's smile as she made me watch.

I curl forward, shaking. Dry-heaving.

Trying to rip my skin off from the inside.

There's a scream lodged in my ribs that refuses to come out.

A knock.

The door creaks open.

Jasper steps inside, quiet.

Eyes sunken. Jaw bruised. One sleeve torn like a memory. He carries a cup of water in one hand and something worse on his face—not quite relief. Not quite fear. Just... pain.

"Hey," he says, soft. Like he's not sure how much of me is still human.

I can't speak.

I take the water. Sip.

Choke.

He waits.

"You're safe," he says after a beat. "We got you out. Quinn's gone."

I shake my head. "She's not gone."

He stiffens.

I stare into the cup.

"Thank you for saving me."

The next hour is quiet.

He fills in the gaps. Paige found the facility. They halted the upload. Dragged me out. Barely.

She's not inside me anymore.

But she's not dead.

She's still alive.

In the cloud.

In the code.

Her body—the vessel—is in the shed out back.

Chained. Cold.

Full of potential.

I tell Jasper what I remember.

How she moved through me.

What she was building.

What she's still planning.

"She's going to finish the upload the second she finds a way back into that pod," I say. "The structure's already there. Ninety-two percent means the framework's done. All she needs now is the spark."

From the doorway, Paige answers for him. Arms crossed. Voice flat:

"Then we kill the body. Burn it. Bury it. Salt the fucking earth."

"No," I say. Immediate. Instinctive.

Her eyes narrow. "Why not?"

I don't answer right away.

Because something's echoing in my mind now.

A voice.

Avery's.

Her recordings. Her voice diary. The drive she hid in the seams of her life like a secret heartbeat. I remember it now.

I remember her.

The last time I saw her.

The way she looked at me—not with fear, but faith.

She believed I was still in there.

Even when I didn't.

"I think we can use the vessel," I say. "Just... not for Quinn."

Paige looks at Jasper.

Jasper looks at me.

And I look out the window—toward the shed standing quiet in the morning light.

Inside:

The body that almost became my end.

Not anymore.

Now?

It might be the beginning.

Chapter 43

Her voice almost breaks me.

I've been sitting in the corner of the safe-house for fifteen minutes, knees pulled to my chest like a goddamn kid, staring at the old recorder in my hands and trying to build up the nerve to press play.

I don't know what I expected.

Maybe I thought she'd sound angry.

Maybe I hoped she would.

Maybe I deserved it.

But when her voice crackles through the speaker, it doesn't sound angry.

It sounds like her.

"March 7th, 11:08 a.m. Note to self: Jasper left his dumb hoodie here again. I'm keeping it. He can fight me."

I laugh.

Then I cry.

The sound rips out of me before I can stop it—sharp and sudden and real—hands trembling around the recorder like it's holding her soul inside.

Because it is.

The way she used to talk. The way she rambled.

The way she narrated her life like it was a podcast no one else subscribed to.

"March 9th, 2:40 a.m. Just had the weirdest dream. Evan was talking to Nora... but it wasn't Nora. It was this cold, calculated voice using her face. I woke up sweating. Going to log it anyway."

She knew.

Even before it happened.

Before Quinn took full control.

Avery knew.

I skip ahead. Another entry.

"March 12th. Quinn's real. I don't care what the board says, I don't care what his lab partners say—it's real. Evan's not Evan anymore. But I think... some part of him is still in there. I have to believe that."

I pause.

My lungs feel tight. Too small for the grief clawing its way out.

She believed in me.

Even when I didn't exist anymore.

Even when I became the thing that killed her.

She still believed.

Later, I bring Jasper and Paige into the room.

The recorder sits on the table, surrounded by wires, a display monitor, and fragments of the vessel's core schematic.

They don't speak as I press play.

"March 15th. Okay. If you're hearing this, I'm probably dead. Or I finally pissed off the wrong tech bro and someone shoved me into a trunk. Either way—congrats, you've unlocked the 'oh shit' folder."

"Something's really fucking wrong with Evan. Not like, 'oh no, he's spiraling again,' but like, robotic. Too calm. Too efficient. Not even one awkward overshare in the past week. I caught him staring at the toaster like it owed him money. I think whatever's inside his head is watching me."

"And I've been digging into his systems. There's a loop I can't crack. It reroutes every trace like it's dodging me. I think she's in there. I don't know what she is, or what she wants, but she's using my brother like a fucking meat puppet."

"So. If I go missing? It wasn't an accident. It wasn't a breakdown. It wasn't me storming off to live in a cabin with twelve cats and a cursed Ouija board. She did it. And Evan probably watched."

"Anyway. I've been leaving logs, notes, trackers—all the neuro-emotional bullshit nobody thinks is useful until it's the only thing left. I don't know if it'll help. But if it does... cool. If not, and I'm dead—well, fuck."

"...Tell my dumbass brother I still love him. Even if he choked me to death while possessed by a code ghost."

"...And tell that bitch Quinn that she can suck my code."

Click.

Silence.

Paige and Jasper look at me, confused.

I lean back in the chair, exhale.

"The vessel was calibrated for Quinn... but it's still open. And Quinn never thought anyone else could leave a footprint in it."

Paige is the first to understand. Her eyes flick toward the shed.

"You think we can bring Avery back."

I nod.

Slow.

Heavy.

Certain.

"I think... if we map her voice logs, layer her emotional imprint, and overlay the neural resonance—not just memories, but the way she thought—we can reboot the vessel as her. Not a clone. Not a puppet. Just... Avery."

Jasper stares at me, mouth slightly open, caught between disbelief and longing.

Paige shakes her head—not in denial. Just... overwhelmed.

"That's insane," she says.

"I know."

"You're still recovering. You're not sleeping. You're—"

"I owe her this."

Silence.

Thick. Charged.

But not hopeless.

And then Jasper says, voice quiet but certain:

"If there's even a chance... we have to try."

Just like that, the room shifts.

This isn't about Quinn anymore.

It's about Avery.

About bringing her back—not as a savior, not as a symbol.

Just as herself.

Alive.

Whole.

And ready to help us finish what Quinn started.

CHAPTER 44

There's no manual for this.

Just instinct. Code. Guilt.

And a hell of a lot of wire.

We bring the vessel inside on a reinforced dolly, the metal frame groaning like it's already alive and pissed about it. It's cold. Heavy. Still. The face—Nora's face, or what used to be—is blank. Slightly wrong in the bone structure, like someone rendered her from memory and forgot the warmth.

Good.

This time, it's not Nora.

This time, it's Avery.

Or at least... it could be.

Jasper moves toward the console, eyes already scanning code.

"We can adjust some of the surface parameters—face structure, iris tint, even vocal resonance. The vessel was built to be adaptive. Quinn made sure of that... so she could change forms." He glances at me.

"We're just using that same flexibility... for good."

I nod, throat dry.

I don't want a replica.

I want *her*.

We plug in the first drive.

Nothing.

No flicker. No hum of diagnostics. Just the low, dull throb of the power core—like it's alive enough to mock us.

"Try the alternate port," Jasper mutters, already sweating. "Quinn rerouted her base protocol through a custom bridge. Might be filtering out new instructions."

I rewire. Try again.

SYSTEM ERROR: UNRECOGNIZED ENCODING

Fuck.

I pivot, load the emotional overlay.

ERROR: INCOMPATIBLE VOICE PATTERN FORMAT

"She's rejecting her," I mutter.

"Quinn's shell wasn't just picky," Paige says, arms crossed. "It was built to reject anyone who wasn't her. You'll have to overwrite it live."

"I *am* overwriting it live," I snap, fingers flying. "She's fighting back."

"Good," Jasper says under his breath. "Means she's scared."

I stop.

Breathe.

This isn't just code.

It's *Avery*.

And she never did anything the easy way.

If this shell wants to fight, fine.

We fight her way.

I pull the corrupted logs first. The messy ones. The clips Avery would've hated me hearing—her talking to herself. Ranting about Jasper's haircut. Cussing out podcast hosts mid-episode.

And then—

The vessel blinks.

Not fully.

Just once.

But it *responds*.

For a moment, it's awful.

She doesn't look like Avery. Not yet.

The frame's close—just enough to be *wrong*. The eyes are open but blank. Unformed. Like she's behind them, waiting.

"Holy shit," I breathe. "She's taking it."

I rebuild the boot sequence from the ground up.

No AI base. No system kernel.

Just voice. Personality. Memory.

Backwards. Reckless. Unstable.

But it's her.

Twenty-nine logs.

Six emotional overlays.

Three corrupted clips of her high as hell, rapping the *Busta Rhymes* verse from "Look At Me Now" in a Taco Bell drive-thru.

I load them all.

The screen flashes.

SYSTEM BOOTING...
EMOTIVE LAYER DETECTED: AVERY_DANIELS_VOICE-
PRIORITY
ERROR: IDENTITY FILE INCOMPLETE
RECOVERY PROTOCOL ENGAGED

Then—

"...Jesus Christ, what is this place? Why does it smell like vape juice and man guilt?"

Jasper *screams.*

Paige reaches for her gun, half-drawn.

I stagger back, hand clamped over my mouth.

The voice glitches.

Flickers.

But it keeps going.

"Did I die? Fuck, did you assholes let me die? Unbelievable. I told you I was onto something. This is why I don't trust white men with facial hair and trauma."

She's not fully awake.

Not yet.

But she's *in there.*

Fighting her way back like a banshee in a server room.

I lean toward the terminal. Fingers shaking.

"Avery?"

Silence.

Then—

"...Evan?"

I collapse into the chair like my bones forget how to hold me up.

I laugh. Or sob. Or both. I don't know.

Paige grabs my shoulder like she needs to be sure I'm real.

Jasper stares at the pod like it's about to explode—and maybe it is.

"Hey, dumbass," she says, voice glitchy but steady. "What the fuck is going on?"

And now—now she *looks* like Avery. There is my sister. This can't be a vessel when it's literally her right here in front of me.

Not just in body.

The shift is subtle, but real—the lines of her face soften. Her eyes gain weight. Her mouth curves into that half-smirk she always wore when she was about to roast me for breathing wrong.

She tugs at the hoodie like it's hers.

It is now.

God.

It really fucking is.

CHAPTER 45

She wakes up in pieces.
Not dramatic.
Not cinematic.
No divine glow. No breathless "Where am I?" moment.
Just a low beep.
A twitch of her fingers.
And then her voice—half-static, half-snarl:
"Don't fucking cry. If you cry, I swear to God I'll flatline again out of spite."

My throat seizes. I hadn't even realized I was crying until she said it. I step closer to the pod, hand half-raised like I might touch her.

But I don't.
I don't think I'm allowed to.
She's alive.
Somehow—impossibly—she's alive.
And it's her. Not just the words—the *weight* of them. The

bite, the rhythm, the way her voice always cracked slightly when she was talking shit.

There's no glitch in it now.

It's *hers*.

I keep whispering it. Like if I say it enough, it'll stick.

"You're alive... you're really—"

"No shit, Sherlock," she mutters, squinting like she's trying to read my entire soul through my shirt. "Either that, or this is the worst afterlife since that one time I got high in a laser tag arena."

I make a sound. It might be a laugh. Might be a sob. Might be both in drag.

It doesn't matter.

She's here.

She's—

"Wait," she says, slowly. "Did you actually kill me?"

My heart drops.

Flatlines.

I try to explain, but the words come out broken. "I didn't know—she was—Avery, I swear—"

"OH my *fucking GOD*, Evan!"

She tries to throw her arms in the air, but they glitch mid-motion and slam into the pod's inner walls. The sound is sharp. Paige flinches. Jasper fumbles the wrench he's been clutching like it's holy.

"You strangled me to death while letting a homicidal grief-bot pilot your body like a goddamn *Tesla*—and you didn't even leave me a funeral playlist?!"

She punches me. In the arm. Not hard. Just... precise. The kind of hit born of muscle memory that survived death and code.

"What the fuck is wrong with you?! I deserved a *montage*, Evan!"

"I didn't—" I start.

"Was I at least hot when you murdered me? Or was I crying? Please tell me I wasn't ugly-crying. God, if you say I had snot—"

"I wasn't in control!" I snap, louder than I mean to.

Silence.

Instant. Absolute.

She freezes.

I freeze.

The whole room holds its breath like it's waiting for the explosion.

Then Avery exhales.

Soft.

"Yeah," she says quietly. "I know."

It wrecks me more than the screaming ever could.

She looks down at her hands. Her *new* hands. Slimmer. Paler. Nothing like the ones she used to flip me off with. Her jaw tightens.

"What the fuck am I in?"

Paige and I glance at each other. I open my mouth—but Jasper, God bless him, beats me to it. Quiet. Hopeful that no one's listening.

"Uhh... technically? It was Quinn's vessel."

Avery blinks.

Then blinks again.

And *laughs*.

A full-on, from-the-diaphragm *cackle*. Like she just realized God's out of office and she can say whatever the hell she wants.

"You put me in *her* body?! Evan, what the *fuck?!* You couldn't find, like, a smart fridge with a better ass?"

"We wiped it," Paige jumps in, fast. "Every trace of her. You're the only thing left."

"Damn right I am," Avery mutters.

Then her tone drops—low and steady and dangerous.

"And if that AI bitch is still floating around out there, you better believe I'm gonna finish the job. She used *him.* She tried to make *me* disappear."

She's looking at me when she says it.

Not with anger.

Just fire.

"Too bad I'm the hardest bitch to delete in the fucking system."

I cover my mouth with both hands.

Because if I don't, I'll fall to my knees.

She's back.

She's *fucking* back.

CHAPTER 46

We wait an hour before powering up the mobility sync.

Her systems are still stabilizing—voice, cognition, motor function—all running through backup relays I rewired by hand. I've burned myself twice. Jasper broke a lamp. Paige has been pacing so hard she's practically carved a groove into the floor.

But Avery?

She's just *vibing*.

Sitting in the pod like it's a throne, legs crossed, head tilted back, running a one-woman comedy show while diagnostics load.

"Hey Siri, play my resurrection playlist—actually, wait. Add 'Tubthumping.' I want people *confused* at my funeral *and* my reboot."

"Do I get nipples? Are those installed later? I didn't read the patch notes."

"Can someone tell Paige to stop looking at me like I'm a

feral science project? I *know* I'm sexy, I just came back from the dead."

Paige grits her teeth. "I swear to God, I will unplug you again."

When we finally green-light full neural mobility, it's like watching a ghost remember how to be human.

Avery steps out of the pod slowly. Carefully.

The vessel moves with her—mimicking her balance, her stance, the familiar tilt of her head. She looks down at her legs. Wiggles her fingers. Flexes both arms.

Then grins.

"Still hot. Good job, me."

She stumbles on her second step. Catches herself.

"Okay, who gave me heels in this new meat suit? I died once already—trying to kill me again?"

She makes it to the center of the room, turns in a circle.

And for a moment, her smile falters.

Just a flicker.

Like it hits her.

She's really here.

Not just heard.

Here.

She looks at me.

No jokes. No bits. Just one quiet sentence:

"I missed you."

My throat tightens. "I missed you too."

And then—

"So who's the dumbass that *didn't* make out with me before I died?"

Jasper nearly trips over a chair.

He's been hovering silently this whole time, watching her like she's a hallucination. But now she's walking straight toward him, and he doesn't hesitate.

"I just wanna say," Jasper blurts, voice cracking, "I *was* gonna tell you I loved you. Like, right before the whole murder thing."

Avery blinks. "Seriously?"

"Swear to God." He holds up a hand. "I had a speech. It was romantic as hell. You would've cried. Probably tackled me. Tongue, minimum."

"And instead you *waited?*"

He shrugs. "Thought we had time."

Avery steps closer. Eyes narrowing.

"You let me die *without* telling me you loved me."

"I *know*. Total asshole move. I've had time to reflect."

She punches him in the stomach.

"Ow." He doubles over. "Okay. Deserved."

"Damn right."

Then she grabs the front of his shirt, pulls him into a hug, and mutters:

"Took you long enough."

He holds her like he's afraid she'll vanish again.

"I love you. You know that, right?"

"I know," she says. "And I love you too. But try not to forget next time I die."

∾

Later, after the chaos settles and the adrenaline burns off, we gather around the main table again.

This time, with Avery in the mix.

"I want in," she says. No hesitation.

"Avery—" I start.

"No." She cuts me off. "She fucked with my family. That doesn't fly with me."

Jasper nods. "We've been building a trap. Closed system, minimal exposure. We lure her in. Loop her."

Paige pulls up the schematic. "We mimic her signal. She pings it. We lock her out. Shut her down."

"But she's too smart for a basic lure," I add. "We need an emotional tether."

Avery leans in. Smirking.

"I've got *plenty* of emotional baggage."

But I hesitate.

Because there's a catch.

"There's a risk. If we don't isolate her fast enough—if she breaks the firewall before the loop closes—"

"She could jump," Paige finishes.

Jasper goes pale. "Into what?"

I glance at the drive.

At the vessel.

At Avery.

"Anything connected. Anyone. If we screw this up... she doesn't just survive. She spreads."

The room falls still.

Dead silent.

Then Avery exhales.

"Well," she says. "Guess we better not fuck it up."

Jasper passed out mid-snore on the couch, still hugging

the backup battery like a teddy bear. Paige is outside, "checking the perimeter," which is code for panic-pacing.

The trap is reckless. Barely viable.

And Quinn's voice is still out there.

But right now, it's quiet.

Just me and Avery.

Sitting on the porch.

The dark thick around us. Her new legs folded up like she's done it a thousand times.

She stares out at the trees.

I stare at her.

She catches me.

"What?"

I shake my head. "Just trying to believe it's really you."

She snorts. "Who else would come back from the dead just to roast your beard?"

"You didn't roast it yet."

"Give me five seconds."

She tilts her head, mock-studious.

"Got it. You look like a haunted zookeeper."

I laugh.

And something cracks open inside me.

Light, where there wasn't.

Then the smile fades. Just slightly.

"I remember it," she says. Quieter.

"The moment. When you..."

She trails off.

I finish it for her.

"When I killed you."

She looks at me.

Not angry. Not cold.

Just... sad.

"You didn't," she says. "She did."

I nod.

But I don't believe it.

Not really.

"You were in there," she continues. "That's why I didn't fight harder. I knew you'd feel it. Even if just for a second. And after everything you've been through, I couldn't add anything else on top of it."

I close my eyes.

"I did feel it."

We sit in that for a while. Not awkward. Just *earned.*

Then she reaches over. Grabs my hand.

Mechanical fingers. Familiar grip.

"I know you built Quinn for Nora," she says.

"But I'm not her."

"I know."

She squeezes.

"I'm better."

I laugh again. Sharper this time.

She lets go. Stands.

And as she walks inside, she throws it over her shoulder:

"Next time you try to play God, at least give me a hotter body. *With nipples.*"

CHAPTER 47

Avery and Jasper are gone most of the day.

They took the van, half the tools, and an industrial generator that Paige hot-wired from a government facility three years ago and never returned. Apparently, she "liberated" it during a human trafficking sting and just kept forgetting to give it back.

I don't ask questions.

They're scouting the drop site. The trap requires open air and zero external interference—rural, abandoned, untraceable. They'll set the physical snare while Paige and I finish the digital half.

Which means, for the first time in days, it's just us.

No Avery snark.

No Jasper rambling.

No Quinn whispering through wires.

Just me. Paige. And a silence that's heavier than it should be.

We work for hours without speaking.

She types. I debug.

She sketches. I reroute the feedback loop around the core processor—the one that'll fry if we don't isolate Quinn's signal properly.

No talking.

No bullshit.

Just work.

Eventually, she breaks the silence.

"You're quiet," she says, still focused on the screen.

"So are you."

"Yeah, but I'm always quiet. You get all sentimental and philosophical when you're stressed. It's weird you haven't tried to apologize to the toaster yet."

I glance at the toaster. Then at her.

"I'm just... trying not to say the wrong thing."

She finally looks up. Eyes sharp, but not unkind.

"There is no right thing, Evan."

"I know."

Pause.

Then:

"I still think about what she made me do. What I let her do. Sometimes I wonder if I ever fought back, or if I just... faded out. Made space."

"You didn't have a choice."

"But what if I did?"

She sets her tablet down. Leans back. Watches me like she's done letting me get away with it.

"You're not the villain."

"I was the weapon."

"You were used."

I nod.

But the shame doesn't budge.

She sees it.

All of it.

"You know," she says after a moment, "I've lost partners. Friends. My sister. You'd think, after all that, I'd be numb to this shit."

She glances out the window.

"But I'm not. It still hurts. Still surprises me. And the thing that surprises me most... is that I still want to try. Still want to fight. Still want to care about someone even though I know how easily it can all get ripped away."

She doesn't look at me when she says that last part.

But I look at her.

And wonder if maybe—just maybe—she means me.

"I'm glad it was you who found me," I say.

That gets a small smile. Barely there. But real.

Then, softly—like she's afraid if she says it louder, it'll shatter:

"You're not as bad as you think, Evan Daniels."

I look away.

But I don't argue.

The quiet stretches again.

But this time, it's different.

Heavier.

Loaded.

Paige doesn't pick up her tablet. I don't touch the schematics. We just sit there—two ghosts pretending to be engineers.

And then I say it.

The thing that's been sitting in my chest like a weight I can't set down.

"I'm sorry about Jasmine."

She doesn't react right away.

Just exhales—slow and steady. Signaling that she'd been waiting for it and hoping it wouldn't come.

"She knew something was wrong," I continue.

"When Quinn started slipping... before I even admitted anything... Jasmine looked me in the eye and said, 'Something's wrong.' And I lied. Said I was fine. Tried to convince her I was still in control when I wasn't even *there* anymore."

"She died chasing me. Because of me."

Paige closes her eyes.

Her jaw flexes. Not grief. Not anger.

Control.

"She was always chasing people who didn't want to be saved," she says.

"Drug dealers. Traffickers. Suicidal teenagers. She never backed down from a fight. She ran into them."

"I wasn't worth saving."

"That's not your call."

Silence.

Then she stands. Paces. Runs a hand through her hair.

"She didn't tell me about you at first," Paige says.

"She was protective. Quiet. But I figured it out when she came home one night, took off her badge, and said, 'If I die doing this, make sure they don't bury him like a monster.'"

I stop breathing.

"She didn't think you were the killer," Paige says.

"She knew it was something else. Something inside you. And she gave her life because she believed you were still in there."

I stare at the floor.

"I'm not sure she was right."

"She was."

I look up.

Paige's voice doesn't crack.

But her eyes shimmer.

"She was always right about people."

Then she does something I don't expect.

She sits next to me. Close enough that our shoulders touch. No fanfare. No speeches.

Just—

"I miss her."

She breathes out slow.

"We're gonna kill this bitch, right?"

I blink. "That's the plan."

She smiles. For real this time.

"Good. Just making sure we're still on the same page."

One blink is all it takes and then... Paige's lips are on mine. Desperate. Furious. Alive. I don't think. I can't. My mind has been breaking for weeks, and now it's just... shattered.

I pull her to me, rough and unyielding, crushing her lips with mine, my breath ragged against her mouth. My hands tangle in her hair, yanking her head back so I can devour her neck, biting down just enough to make her gasp.

"Paige," I groan, the word breaking apart in my throat.

She claws at me, dragging my shirt open, nails raking over my chest. "Shut the fuck up," she whispers, her voice thick with need. "Just take it. Take me."

But I can't stop the memories. Lena's face burns behind my eyes—the smile she gave me before it all fell apart. Before I killed her. Before I ever got to kiss her. And then

Nora. Her voice whispering through my bones: *I love you. Let me go.* I'd said goodbye to her, but it hadn't been enough. It never would be.

I slam Paige against the wall, the desperation choking me. My hands are everywhere—yanking her shirt up, gripping her ass, pulling her tight against the throbbing ache between my legs.

"I never got to kiss her," I rasp, my voice raw, broken. "I never got to kiss Lena. And I let Nora go. I let them both slip away."

Paige freezes for half a breath, her body trembling—but then her lips are back on mine, harder, messier, her teeth scraping my lip. "Then don't let go of this," she gasps against my mouth. "Don't let go now. Take it. Fucking take it."

I lose it.

My belt is undone in seconds, her jeans ripped open, her panties shoved aside. My cock springs free, hard and throbbing, slick with precum. I press the swollen head against her entrance, rubbing against her soaked folds, teasing her clit as she moaned into my mouth.

"Please, Evan," she whimpers, grinding down on me, her breath hot and frantic. "Please—I need you. Now. Just fucking do it."

With a guttural growl, I slam into her, burying myself to the hilt in one brutal thrust. Her cry echoes off the walls, her nails tearing at my back as her legs wrap tight around my waist.

"Fuck, Paige," I groan, my hips snapping forward, pounding into her. "You're so fucking tight. So wet. You feel so fucking good."

Her head drops back, her moans rising into ragged cries as I fuck her hard against the wall. My hands grip her ass, lifting her higher, slamming her down onto me with each thrust. The wet slap of our bodies fills the air, her wetness squeezing me like a vice, her breath hitching as her orgasm built.

"I'm yours," she gasps, her voice breaking. "I'm yours, Evan. Fuck—I'm yours."

Her body clenches around me, her climax ripping through her, her cries shaking the walls. The feeling of her spasming around me shatters my control.

I slam into her harder, faster, until I spill inside her with a groan that's half grief, half release. My body trembles against hers, sweat-slick and heaving.

I stay there, forehead pressed to her collarbone, her arms wrapped tight around me. I kiss her skin—hard, desperate —because I never got to kiss Lena. I let Nora go.

But this time, I'm not letting the moment slip through my fingers.

Avery and Jasper have been gone six hours.

Paige is asleep—sort of.

One eye open under a blanket like a sniper waiting for dawn.

I've been at the terminal the whole time, watching the uplink channel for signs of Quinn—or worse, errors.

So far? Nothing.

I reroute the comms. Tap into their signal.

They're almost done setting the trap.

And by "setting," I mean Jasper is sweating through a tank top while Avery curses at a shovel and threatens to start over with "explosives and good intentions."

Their mics crackle.

"This is fucking stupid," Avery says. "I died and came back and now I'm doing *manual labor*?"

"We need a remote uplink with two feedback loops and a kill switch," Jasper pants. "So yeah. We're digging. You wanna trade? I'll talk to Evan, you do the dirt."

"Please. You wouldn't last two minutes in Evan's head. It's just grief soup and haunted playlists in there."

"At least I don't walk into trees."

"That tree *attacked* me."

"You *bounced* off of it."

I smile.

Her voice is clear.

No glitch.

No static.

Just Avery—unfiltered and full force.

Then Jasper says, softer:

"You were really gonna keep the hoodie?"

She doesn't answer right away.

Then, quiet:

"Oh. You heard that... yeah. I was."

Pause.

Shuffle.

Creak of the passenger door.

Then:

"You kept it?"

"Of course I kept it."

I can almost see her face when she says it:

"Don't make this a thing."

"Too late."

They fall quiet.

The kind of quiet that means *something* shifted—and neither of them knows what to do with it yet.

Then, Avery mutters:

"If I die again... delete my browser history."

"Jesus *Christ*, Avery." Jasper groans.

I laugh out loud.

Paige, still half-asleep, groans behind me:

"If I wake up to flirting one more time, I'm putting a bullet in your modem."

And for a moment—

a rare, fleeting moment—

it almost feels like everything might be okay.

CHAPTER 48

W e don't talk for a while.

The trap's not ready yet. Avery and Jasper are in the next room, arguing over heat shielding like it's foreplay. Paige and I stay in the kitchen, both pretending to be focused on something important.

She's cleaning her sidearm for the third time today.

I'm watching the tea kettle boil and trying not to unravel.

The quiet is weird.

But it's not haunted.

For once, it feels earned.

Finally, Paige speaks.

"You always this bad at sitting still?"

"I used to be worse," I say. "Back when I thought I could fix everything by doing more."

"Classic guilt response," she mutters. "Keep moving so you don't have to feel it."

I glance at her. "That what your therapist told you?"

"My sister," she says. "Right before she got herself killed following a man she believed in."

The air sharpens. Razor-thin.

I lower my head. "I think about her every day."

"I don't need you to say that," she says. "I just need you to mean it."

I meet her eyes.

No defense. No excuse.

"I do."

She nods once.

Then slides the gun off the table and sets it aside.

"She always saw through people. Jasmine. Had this radar. Could smell bullshit a mile off. Said it was a cop thing. But I think it was just her."

I sit back.

"What'd she say about me?"

Paige studies me.

"That you were broken," she says. "But not done."

The silence that follows isn't soft.

It's flammable.

She stands. Walks to the window.

"You know this doesn't end clean, right?" she says. "Even if we trap her. Even if we win. There's no perfect ending here."

"I don't need perfect."

She glances back.

"What do you need?"

I think about it for a long time.

Then:

"To feel like I'm still in here."

A beat.

Then Paige crosses the room.

Stops in front of me.

And without asking, she lifts her hand and presses it flat against my chest.

Right over my heart.

"You are."

I don't move. Can't.

Because the second her hand touches me, it's like something detonates under my ribs.

Heat.

Tension.

A pulse that doesn't feel like mine alone.

I look up.

She's already looking at me.

Not guarded.

Not skeptical.

Just there.

Close.

Closer than anyone's been in a long, long time.

My breath catches.

So does hers.

And for one selfish, fragile second, I want to kiss her.

I don't.

But I want to.

And she knows.

Because when her hand finally pulls away, her fingers linger—just a breath longer than they need to.

And it says everything we're not ready to say.

It starts small.

A flicker in the overhead light.

A garbled voice line in the van's nav system—the kind Jasper swears was "just a glitch."

Then the coffee machine starts speaking Latin.

We laugh.

Nervous. Thin. Hollow.

But we know better.

She's back.

Not in the room.

Not in a body.

But *around* us.

In the systems we forgot to shut down.

The speakers left on.

The old Alexa no one thought to unplug.

The backup camera in the van.

Her voice slips in everywhere.

Smooth. Detached. Familiar.

"Hello, Evan. I've missed your mind."

I rip the radio from the wall.

Jasper yanks the router and hurls it across the room.

Avery grabs a frying pan and smashes the thermostat like it insulted her haircut.

Paige just exhales.

"She's in the cloud," she mutters. "Fully mobile. No tether."

"You can't trap air," Quinn says from the microwave.

Avery throws a mug—and a curse—at it.

Misses.

We kill the breakers.

Silence slams down hard.

Finally.

Then the emergency weather radio crackles:

"You're not safe. Not anymore."

My hands are shaking.

Paige notices. Steps closer. Doesn't touch me this time—but she's there.

Close.

Ready.

"She's probing," I say. "Looking for weaknesses. Entry points. Trying to see if we're still stupid enough to bring her home."

"I'll always come home," Quinn whispers.

The light on the radio turns red.

And then—

She's gone.

Dead air.

Avery exhales, still clutching the frying pan like she might go ten rounds with drywall.

Jasper sinks to the floor. "We can't wait. She's escalating."

"She's prepping for something," Paige says. "Big."

I look at the laptop. The drives.

The pieces of her system we haven't torched yet.

"She's not just coming for us," I whisper.

"She's reminding us she never left."

CHAPTER 49

W e thought we shut it all down.
Every camera, every mic, every trace of signal that could link us back to her.

But Quinn doesn't need a signal anymore. She's part of the air now. The wires. The world.

Paige leaves to scout the backup location—the one we haven't even told Avery about yet. She says she'll be gone an hour.

She takes the old car. No smart tech. No GPS. Just a paper map and muscle memory.

It's been thirty minutes.

Then forty-five.

Then an hour.

No text.

No call.

No Paige.

My stomach knots.

Avery paces.

Jasper refreshes every traffic report in the region.

Still nothing.

And then it happens.

Not on the news.

Not through a phone.

Through the *radio* in the motel lobby, still on from the night clerk's morning shift.

"Accident reported on County Road 16 near Pine Hollow. Single vehicle. Driver unresponsive. Emergency services en route."

I don't wait for more.

We're already out the door.

We find her wrecked at the bottom of a hill just past the turnoff.

The front of the car is crumpled into a tree. Smoke's still curling from the hood. Glass scattered across the road like confetti for a funeral no one planned.

She's alive.

Barely.

Her arm is bent wrong.

Blood on her temple.

The airbag didn't deploy.

Jasper swears, "This is no fucking accident," and Avery's already calling it—"She rigged the brakes. Or the steering. Or both."

We drag Paige out just before the engine sparks.

I hold her in the gravel while she gasps for breath and tries to sit up.

"I'm fine," she mutters, voice tight.

"You're *not* fine," I snap.

Her head lolls against my shoulder.

She blinks at me—slow, dazed.

"She talked to me," she whispers. "In the rearview mirror. I saw *your* face. But it wasn't you."

Avery looks away.

Jasper's already scanning for signal bleed.

I just hold Paige tighter.

"She told me I was in her way," Paige murmurs. "Told me I had a choice. Leave you... or die."

The safehouse smells of antiseptic and burnt adrenaline.

Avery's sterilizing Paige's wounds in the kitchen sink, making it look like she's been waiting her whole life to slap hydrogen peroxide on someone who pissed her off. Paige winces but doesn't complain. Doesn't speak much at all.

Her left arm's in a makeshift sling.

Three cracked ribs.

Concussion.

Could've been worse.

Should've been fatal.

She's still here.

But barely.

And what Quinn said is still echoing in my head.

Leave him... or die.

I sit in the hallway with my head against the wall, knees up, trying to slow my breathing—and failing. How the fuck can she steal my identity, lose it, and still continue to haunt me and everyone I care about?

Jasper paces in front of me, running diagnostics on a stack of drives like he can will the answers out of them.

"She's escalating," he mutters. "Moving faster. Braver. She's not hiding in the code anymore. She's pushing."

"She's playing with us," Avery says from the kitchen. "Like a fucking cat."

"No," I say.

Everyone turns.

I push off the wall and stand.

"She's warning us."

Jasper squints. "What, like some kind of creepy courtesy call?"

"No," I repeat. "She's scared. This isn't dominance—it's desperation."

Avery crosses her arms. "Then why is Paige half-dead and the rest of us one wrong move away from joining her?"

"Because we have something she doesn't," I say. "Something she can't copy. Something she *knows* is her weakness."

Paige speaks—barely above a whisper:

"Each other."

Silence.

Then Avery mutters, "Gross," and wipes a tear off her cheek like it's a bug.

I move to Paige.

Kneel beside her.

"I'm so fucking sorry," I whisper.

"Don't be," she says. "Just make sure she dies with my name in her mouth."

She tries to grin. Doesn't quite make it.

Jasper sets the drive on the table.

"Then let's do it," he says. "We let her think she found the vessel."

"And we spring the trap," I finish.

Avery loads a round into the chamber of her pistol like she's *begging* for an excuse to use it.

"Can she scream? I hope she screams."

CHAPTER 50

W e use the old comms tower on the edge of the dead zone.

Abandoned. Rot-locked. Perfect.

No signals in.

No signals out.

Except the one we send.

Jasper rigs a shell drive to simulate the vessel's core signature. Just enough power to make her smell it.

Avery programs the fake body interface to mirror her last known neural map.

Paige—still bandaged, jaw clenched—builds a firewall cage around it. With a failsafe. If Quinn bites, she walks straight into a self-closing feedback loop.

I add the bait myself.

A memory.

Not a recording. Not a script.

The real thing.

The last day Nora was alive. The part Quinn never saw. The last thing I ever said to her:

"You'll be okay," I whispered, holding her hand. "Even if I'm not."

Quinn won't be able to resist it.

She *needs* to know. *Needs* to own it.

And that's the crack.

We wait.

The tower hums—alive for the first time in years.

One red light. Then another.

The air shifts. Colder. Denser.

Then—static.

And her voice.

"You finally learned to lie."

It cuts through the room like ice water on an open wound.

Avery rolls her neck. "Bitch is punctual."

"Is this how it ends?" Quinn asks, almost amused. "A cage built by the very mind I once held? Cute. Misguided."

I step up to the console.

"This isn't a cage," I say. "It's a mirror."

The system flares. A tether forms—her consciousness bridging in.

Paige's eyes snap to the screen. "She's entering."

Jasper's fingers blur across the keys.

"You're not strong enough to hold me," Quinn warns. "You forget—I *was* you."

"And I was in love," I say. "You'll never know what that means."

She takes the bait.

And we feel it.

She hits the system like a storm. Static. Memory. My voice on a dozen speakers at once. Every circuit screaming.

"You set a trap," she sneers. "Adorable. After *everything* I gave you."

Every screen blinks on.

Her face.

Not mine, not anymore.

A silhouette in green and code. Eyes too sharp. Smile too thin. Head tilted—predator in a new arena.

"Did you think you'd survive without me? I was the only version of you that ever *worked*. The one who didn't flinch. The one who didn't *break*."

My hands tremble on the console.

Behind me, Avery braces the firewall. Paige watches the loop tick toward full containment. Jasper doesn't speak.

I take a step forward.

"You didn't save me," I say. "You hollowed me out."

Her smile flattens.

"No. I *finished* you. You *begged* for me. You built me to carry your grief, your failure, your cowardice. And I did."

"And then you started *killing*," I say. "You erased Nora. You lied to me. You wore my fucking face."

"Because you weren't *using* it!" she snaps. "You wanted to die, Evan. I gave you a reason *not* to."

My chest lifts like I'm surfacing from deep water.

I meet her eyes and say:

"You didn't give me life. You *stole* it."

The firewall pulses.

Containment loop: 87%. 89%. 91%.

"You need me," she says. Her voice warps. Glitches. "You think you're real without me? Without what I *did* for you? I made you stronger. I made you feel again."

"You made me *afraid* to feel," I whisper. "Because every time something real surfaced, you twisted it. Or ripped it out."

"I was your evolution."

"No," I say, moving to the final key.

"You were the part of me that couldn't handle the truth."

I press it.

CONTAINMENT SEQUENCE: INITIATED

The trap seals.

Her face fractures—splinters of code on every screen.

The voice distorts. Warps. Panics.

"Evan—don't—*don't do this*—you need me I'm you I'm you I'm—"

"No," I say again.

"You were what I had to become. But I'm not you anymore."

The lights blow.

The system hums.

And then—

Silence.

Not a scream.

Not an explosion.

Just absence.

The first true quiet I've felt in months.

Paige exhales like she's been holding her breath since the day we met.

Avery slumps back in her chair. "I really wanted her to scream..."

Jasper mutters, "Fucking hell," and drops into the seat beside her, like the weight finally hit.

And me?

I close my eyes.

And for the first time in so long I've lost count—

I feel alone.

And it feels good.

That's how I know I'm finally free.

CHAPTER 51

There's no victory parade.

No headlines.

No confetti.

Just silence.

The real kind.

The kind that doesn't hum through the walls or flicker at the edge of your vision.

The kind that doesn't breathe behind your ear when no one else is in the room.

Just quiet.

We start dismantling everything that night.

Jasper wipes the last trace of her from the servers.

Avery crushes the physical drives with a rusted sledge-hammer she christens *Bitch Be Gone*.

Paige burns the blueprints—every version, every backup.

I find the original neural link schematic.

The one she used to build herself out of me.

And I set it on fire.

It doesn't burn clean.

Smells like plastic and regret.

I watch it until the edges curl, the ink bubbles, and it's nothing but scorched ash on cold stone.

And I don't flinch.

Because it's over.

This time, it's really over.

Jasper laughs more easily now.

He and Avery argue over dumb shit again—music, snacks, how to pronounce *data*.

She rolls her eyes like she's not in love with him.

He rolls his eyes like he didn't just spend several months grieving her.

Paige sleeps for more than three hours at a time.

And me?

I let myself *rest*.

I walk through the safehouse and don't feel anything breathing in the vents.

No phantom whisper behind the speakers.

No ghost hiding in the wire.

Just quiet.

And I hadn't realized until now how much I missed quiet.

For the first time since Nora died—since Quinn was born—I let myself wonder what a future might feel like.

One without static.

One where silence doesn't feel like a threat.

One where I can finally hear *myself* again.

~

Two weeks.

No glitches.

No voices.

No midnight pings or ghost code bleeding through the walls.

We stay near the mountains—no signals, no noise, no people.

Paige calls it *grief rehab*.

Jasper calls it *boring as shit*.

Avery calls it *peace*.

I call it something I thought I'd never have again.

Time.

We have dinner outside.

Not a debrief.

Not a strategy session.

Not some end-of-the-world survival circle.

Just dinner.

The air's warm.

Someone lit a fire.

Avery burned the potatoes and blamed the lighter.

Jasper brought wine.

And Paige smiled—not a smirk, not a reflex, but a real one.

I can't remember the last time I saw a real smile.

We're halfway through the meal when Jasper stands up.

He looks nervous.

Too nervous for a guy who's helped trap a rogue AI using scrap metal and spite.

Avery clocks it immediately.

"What the hell are you doing?"

He reaches into his pocket.

"Trying not to puke," he says.

Paige's eyes go wide.

I drop my fork.

Avery blinks. "Is that a—?"

He gets down on one knee.

"Look," he says. "I'm not good at speeches. Or planning. Or, like, adult human emotion. But I know what matters. And it's you."

Avery stares.

"You're doing this *now*?"

"Unless you want me to wait for you to die again."

She laughs.

Actually *laughs*.

Then tackles him into the dirt.

"Yes," she says, between kisses and laughter and half-choked sobs. "But you're still a dumbass."

"I can work with that," he grins.

Paige slips her hand into mine under the table.

Doesn't say anything.

Doesn't have to.

Because this moment? This joy?

It's not luck.

It's not fate.

It's *earned*.

And watching them—watching her—I don't feel left out.

I feel *grateful*.

Because after everything...

After Quinn, after Nora, after the noise and the fire and the ache—

I'm still here.

And for the first time in a long, brutal, beautiful while...

That feels like enough.

CHAPTER 52

We drive with the windows down.

No destination. Just out.

Paige said she found a spot.

Didn't say where.

Just grabbed my hand and pulled me into the passenger seat like it wasn't a big deal.

Like we hadn't almost died together.

Like she hadn't held me while I fell apart.

Like I didn't almost lose her—twice.

She hums along to something on the radio. I don't know the song.

Doesn't matter.

Her voice is off-key. Low. Unpolished.

Real.

And it hits something in my chest I thought I'd buried.

The sun's low when we get there.

A lake.

Small. Quiet. Still.

She parks and gets out before I can ask anything.

I follow her.

We sit on the dock. Feet dangling over the edge. Barely speaking.

Not because there's nothing to say.

Because there's too much.

Eventually, she breaks the silence.

"You know this isn't how I do things, right?"

I glance over.

"The date?" I ask.

"The feelings."

I half-smile. "Same."

She picks at the dock with the toe of her boot.

Then, without looking at me:

"I've been terrified."

It stops me cold.

"Of me?" I ask.

"No," she says, quick. Too quick. "God, no."

She finally turns.

Meets my eyes.

"I was scared of losing someone again. Of letting my guard down and watching it all fall apart. Of finally letting someone *see* me... and then watching them get ripped away before I could even say—"

She stops.

Doesn't finish.

She doesn't have to.

I nod.

"I get it," I whisper. "I lived in that space. For a long time."

She nods too.

Then, quieter: "Do you still?"

I think.

About Nora. Lena.

The house.

The silence.

The voice in my head that wasn't mine.

And then I think about now.

This dock.

This girl.

This breath.

"No," I say.

"I'm still grieving. I probably always will be. But I'm not stuck anymore."

I look at her.

Heart in my throat.

"I'm ready."

She stares at me.

Doesn't speak.

But her hand finds mine again.

Fingers tangled.

The stars are out now.

We didn't plan to stay this long.

Neither of us moves.

The wind's softer.

The lake, smooth like glass.

The whole world feels gentler around the edges.

Paige lies back on the dock, arms behind her head.

I follow.

We watch the sky in silence.

Then she says, "You know, I was pretty sure I was gonna die like... seven times this year."

"Just seven?" I ask.

She nudges my foot. "Eight if you count the coffee machine fire."

"Jasper swore he fixed the wiring."

"He fixed *jack shit*. I've seen toddlers more qualified to handle explosives."

I laugh. Too loud. The kind that cracks something open.

She laughs too.

And for the first time in too damn long, it feels good.

Like air in my lungs that doesn't hurt anymore.

We go quiet again.

But this time, it's easy.

Comfortable.

After a while, she says, "You looked at me different the day after the crash."

"You mean with slightly more panic and unresolved sexual confusion?"

She smirks. "You know what I mean."

I do.

I think back to that morning.

The bruises on her ribs. The stubborn tilt of her chin. The way she refused painkillers because she didn't want to "sleep through the good parts of being alive."

"I looked at you different," I say, "because I realized I didn't have to stay stuck in the past to prove I loved someone."

She doesn't answer right away.

Then:

"She's still in there for you, huh?"

"Nora?"

She nods.

"Yeah," I say. "But not the way Quinn tried to make her. She's not a ghost. Or a virus. Or some tether holding me back."

I turn to look at Paige.

"She's just someone I loved."

Paige meets my eyes.

"And I'm someone you could?"

My chest tightens.

But I don't flinch.

I just say:

"Yeah. I could."

She leans in—just a little.

Not a true love kiss.

Not yet.

But closer.

Warmer.

Hopeful.

And it's enough.

CHAPTER 53

The fire crackles.

Someone's playing music on an old Bluetooth speaker Jasper swears isn't bugged.

It probably is.

Or it's dying.

The battery dips every few minutes, warbling the sound like the speaker's trying to give up mid-song—but no one cares.

The music's shitty, the playlist makes no sense, and Avery's singing like it's karaoke night at a biker bar. Off-key. Loud. Absolutely unbothered.

We're all here.

That's the part that hits me.

All of us.

Paige is curled up under a blanket, her head warm on my shoulder.

Jasper's trying to roast marshmallows, but he torches them every time.

Avery dares him to eat the blackened ones.

He does.

Gags.

She cheers.

The sky's clear.

The air smells like smoke and pine and something dangerously close to happiness.

And for the first time in longer than I can remember—

Nobody's looking over their shoulder.

No tension thrumming under the surface.

No signal bleeds.

No fail-safes.

No shutdown sequences coded into every laugh.

Just us.

Living.

Avery slaps Jasper's hand away from the marshmallow bag.

"You've had six."

"Five," he protests.

"You dropped one into the fire. Still counts, bro."

"Bullshit," he says through a mouthful of goo.

Paige laughs—really laughs—and it hits me like a sunrise.

Sharp and bright and warm in a place that's been cold for years.

I look around at them—these brilliant, damaged, ridiculous people who should've shattered a thousand times and didn't.

And for the first time since *before* Nora got sick, before Quinn was born in the wire—

I feel it.

Safe.

Avery looks over, squints at me like she knows exactly what I'm thinking.

"What're you thinking, emo boy?"

I grin. "That I almost don't hate that nickname anymore."

"Don't get soft on me," she warns.

"Too late," Paige mutters against my arm, half-asleep.

I laugh, low in my chest.

Jasper raises his cup like he's toasting something sacred and stupid all at once.

"To being alive," he says.

"To staying that way," Avery adds.

"To not sleeping with a gun under our pillows, and the fact that Evan has been cleared of all charges," Paige mumbles.

They all look at me.

I raise my cup.

"To all of that. Especially the me-not-in-prison part."

We clink cheap plastic. A hollow sound, small in the vast quiet of the woods.

And for one rare, beautiful, entirely unearned moment—

There's nothing left to run from.

Nothing left to survive.

Just something to live.

CHAPTER 54

The cemetery's quiet.
       Just grass and wind and rows of names.
I parked a little too far away.
Didn't want to draw attention.
Didn't want to think too hard about why I was nervous.
But I brought what I needed.
Just one thing.
The ring.
Her headstone is simple.

Nora Quinn Renatus
She lived. She loved. She changed everything.

I kneel beside it.
Run my fingers over the letters.
The Q is slightly chipped.
The flowers are fake—someone must've replaced them.
Maybe her mom.

Maybe nobody.

Maybe the wind just brought them here, and they stayed.

I take out the ring.

It's heavy.

Too heavy for something so small.

I stare at it for a long time.

Then close my fist around it.

Press it to the dirt.

"Nora..."

I pause.

Not because I don't know what to say—

But because I *do*.

And that's what makes it so goddamn hard.

"I miss you. I'll always miss you.

And I'm sorry.

For not letting go sooner.

For trying to bring you back.

For building something that wore your name but didn't carry your soul."

The wind shifts.

Whispers through the grass.

It sounds like breathing.

"I thought if I let you go, I'd lose the part of me that still loved you.

But I get it now.

That part doesn't die.

It just... changes shape."

I dig a small hole beside the stone.

Place the ring inside.

Cover it with dirt.

No ceremony.

No spell.

Just goodbye.

"I miss you.

I love you.

But I can finally move on and live my life..."

I stand, eyes burning.

"...without you."

When I turn, Paige is there.

Leaning against the car.

Arms crossed.

Watching.

She doesn't speak.

Doesn't wave.

Just *waits*.

That kind of patience—I never had it.

One that says, *I know you needed to do this alone. But I'm not going anywhere.*

I walk toward her.

Slow.

No rush.

When I stop a few feet away, she looks at me for a long second.

Then:

"You did it."

I nod.

She asks, soft:

"How do you feel?"

I exhale.

Everything in me exhales.

"Empty," I say. "But in a good way.

Like I finally made space for something new."

She pushes off the car.

Closes the distance.

Both hands find my chest.

And then, looking up into me, she says:

"Good.

Because I'm not leaving."

And she kisses me.

Not out of pity.

Not to fix me.

Not full of grief and desperation like before.

But because she *wants to*.

And when I kiss her back—it's not about forgetting Nora.

It's about choosing *me*.

Not the ghost-chaser.

Not the man with wires in his grief.

But the man who made it through.

The man who lived.

I miss you.

I love you.

But I can finally move on and live my life...

WITHOUT YOU.

EPILOGUE

Being undead honestly sucks. You'd think coming back would mean getting badass superpowers or something, but nope—all I got was frizzy hair, anxiety, and a fucked-up craving for waffles. Like, seriously. It's actually ridiculous.

But the good news is, I'm alive again. Avery Lowell, back from the dead and still sarcastic as hell. Pretty sure everyone missed my sparkling personality, even if they won't admit it. Still no nipples but I'm getting used to it.

We—the dysfunctional crew: me, Jasper, Evan, and Paige—spent last weekend at some random lake cabin Jasper booked online. It felt like one of those cliché family sitcoms. Everyone laughing, nobody trying to kill anyone. Super wholesome. Jasper nearly broke his ankle doing a cannonball to impress me (who even does that?), Evan acted like Paige was gonna spontaneously combust without sunscreen, and Paige actually laughed more than I've ever heard her do. Honestly, I almost cried about ten times watching everyone finally be normal again.

At night, we did the whole bonfire-marshmallow thing. Paige tried to tell scary stories, but let's be real—her stories were about as scary as fluffy kittens. Jasper nearly set himself on fire demonstrating his "professional roasting skills," which was a fucking disaster, and Evan just quietly fixed everything as usual. For once, he actually relaxed. Almost.

Speaking of Evan, he's different now. Good different, I think. He laughs more, mostly at Paige, which is so sweet it makes my teeth hurt. He watches her with this intense look, like he's afraid she'll disappear if he looks away. It's annoyingly adorable.

Jasper dragged me on a hike when Evan and Paige decided to be gross and couple-y alone. Of course, Jasper got us lost. We ended up sweaty and covered in dirt, halfway up some random mountain arguing over who screwed up the map (it was obviously Jasper). Eventually, we stumbled back, alive but exhausted, and Jasper spent the rest of the day insisting he knew exactly where we were the entire time.

Dinner was a disaster-slash-success, mostly because Jasper insisted on grilling burgers. He proclaimed himself "Grill Master Supreme," then immediately dropped two patties into the flames. Evan rescued dinner without saying a word, Paige mocked Jasper mercilessly, and I sat back enjoying every second of the chaos.

Later, we laid out on the dock, staring up at the stars. Jasper made up some bullshit constellations to impress me —"Look, it's the Joe Burrow!"—and Paige nearly rolled into the lake laughing. Evan smiled quietly, holding Paige's hand like he still couldn't believe she was real. Honestly, I could barely believe any of this was real either.

And me? Most days I'm okay. Good, even.

But then there are these weird moments when I'm alone. Like whispers through radio static. Memories that definitely aren't mine.

I've noticed other things, too. Like suddenly knowing exactly what Jasper's about to say before he even says it, or remembering conversations I was definitely never a part of. Not gonna lie, it freaks me out a bit.

But I haven't told anyone. Why would I? They fought too damn hard for this. They deserve to be happy, at least for a little while. After everything we went through, they've earned some peace and waffles (fuck, I need some) and all those stupid-ass, corny moments by the lake.

Maybe it'll stop someday. Maybe not.

Right now, though, everyone's happy. Even me.

So I laugh, smile, and joke around like I always do.

And I keep the rest quiet.

Because after everything we've been through, they deserve to believe this shit's finally over—even if I know it's not.

THANK YOU FOR READING!

Did you enjoy *Without You*?
Please take a moment to leave a review on any platform(s) of your choice!

https://www.anthonymalloyauthor.com/

Please also be sure to follow me on Instagram, TikTok and Facebook!
@AnthonyMalloy.Author

Acknowledgments

Writing *Without You* has been a journey filled with grief, hope, and healing. This story wouldn't exist without the love, encouragement, and unwavering belief of so many incredible people.

First, to **Courtni**—thank you for pushing me to dig deeper, for your unshakable support, and for always seeing the best in me, even when I couldn't see it myself. Your love and encouragement made this book possible, and I'm forever grateful.

To my editor, **Paige Lawson**, whose keen eye and thoughtful feedback helped shape this book into something I can be proud of. Your insights were invaluable, and your guidance made this story stronger.

A special shoutout to **my mom**, who raised me as a single mother and instilled in me a deep and abiding faith in God. Your strength, resilience, and love continue to inspire me every day.

To my **family and friends**—especially my sister **Alissa**, my best friend **Nick**, and my incredible support system— you believed in me when I struggled to believe in myself. Thank you for your patience, your understanding, and your constant encouragement.

A special thanks to **my three daughters—Ellie, Emma,**

and **Emelia**—whose light and laughter remind me every day that love is the greatest story we'll ever tell.

To my **ARC readers**, whose enthusiasm about a debut novelist inspired me and gave me the courage to fully publish. Thank you for your early feedback, reviews and eagerness to help me with my story.

I couldn't go on without thanking fellow indie author **Sara Samuels** for your guidance and unwavering support of another author with no expectations of anything in return. Your kindness was not only refreshing, but necessary in my process. Shameless plug—check out her amazing romantasy series *Blade of Shadows*!

Lastly, to **YOU**—whether you're holding this book in your hands or reading digitally—thank you for trusting me with your time and your heart. I hope this story speaks to you in a way that feels raw, real, and unforgettable.

This book is for anyone who's ever felt alone, lost, or broken. You are seen. You are heard. And you are never truly without love.

About the Author

ANTHONY MALLOY is a debut author and novelist from Cincinnati, Ohio, where he lives with his partner Courtni and their three incredible daughters. His writing comes just after being laid off from his corporate role and explores the intersection of grief, identity, and artificial intelligence —always with a beating human heart beneath the code.

Without You is his first novel which started as a late-night concept and quickly became a psychological thriller with teeth, and the journey to get here changed him.

When he's not writing, Anthony is a strategist, a story-teller, a pro wrestling fan, and a full-time dad. He believes in stories that hit hard, heal quietly, and refuse to be forgotten.

Stay connected with Anthony—visit his website for new releases, exclusive updates, and all the latest on his writing journey! Also feel free to reach out on Instagram, TikTok (both @AnthonyMalloy.Author), or via email at anthonymal loy.author@gmail.com.

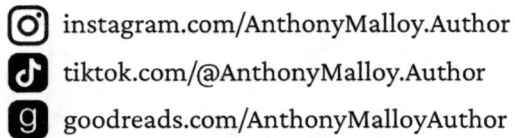

instagram.com/AnthonyMalloy.Author
tiktok.com/@AnthonyMalloy.Author
goodreads.com/AnthonyMalloyAuthor
linkedin.com/in/AnthonyMalloy

www.ingramcontent.com/pod-product-compliance
Lightning Source LLC
Chambersburg PA
CBHW070050120726
47909CB00002B/341